Abo

Born in Laurenzana (in the Italian boot's ankle), I came to America around Christmas 1953. After studying Italian, Latin and Greek for thirteen years, I found English a most illogical subject at De Paul University where I earned a BA before joining the US Army in 1958. The GI Bill helped me attain a Master's in '64 and my PhD in '74 at Loyola University while teaching English to American students at Wright College in Chicago. I retired forty years later (sixteen as English Department Head). Life is full of delicious ironies, don't you find?

I have edited scientific books, Italian-American magazines, written songs, poems, short stories, a play, and three novels. My Italian poems were published in

The father of five, I coached soccer teams, Boy Scouts, women's karateka, and yet enjoyed playing cards and coffee klatches with my Italian-, German-, French-, and Spanish-speaking American friends. I am *still* trying to solve one *New York Times* Crossword Puzzle.

FLORIO AND BIANCOFIORE:
PERIPATETIC LOVERS

Rocco Blasi

FLORIO AND BIANCOFIORE: PERIPATETIC LOVERS

Vanguard Press

A CIP catalogue record for this title is
available from the British Library.

ISBN 9781784657-61 1

*Vanguard Press is an imprint of
Pegasus Elliot MacKenzie Publishers Ltd.*
www.pegasuspublishers.com

First Published in 2020

**Vanguard Press
Sheraton House Castle Park
Cambridge England**

Printed & Bound in Great Britain

Dedication

This book is dedicated first of all to Joyce Blasi, my multi-talented wife for nearly half a century, who wrote down my dictations—in artful calligraphy that saved me hundreds of trips to the typist—and still managed to raise beautiful and successful children—Rocky, Tasha, Rosa, Marina and Michael—and babysit for grandchildren Liv, Lucia, Hudson, Mila and Kaia. I also dedicate this book to my parents and siblings (all gone, but Tina), my Wright colleagues and students, veterans, neighbours and *paesani* everywhere. After all I gladly dedicate it to you, **my readers**—the main reason for its existence.

PREAMBLE

This story takes place in the middle of the eighth century, when holy wars (the oldest oxymoron and excuse for incursions and territorial expansions) in the name of diverse social and religious cleansing were uprooting people, cultures, and social orders.

It was a time when Old Tenets were being replaced by New Laws, but not easily or quickly or popularly. As always, people are not eager to change traditions, familiar or familial places, rituals or rites, customs or ethos imposed by outside forces or religious fiats. They may swear allegiance to a new king or god, but in their heart the replacement does not occur readily... and the gods removed do not necessarily go away because they are banned by decree, fashion, or even charismatic evangelisation.

Beliefs were adapted more easily than adopted. New (Roman) names were given to old (Greek) icons. Pagan temples often became churches or mosques. Religious entities representing Good and Evil changed nominally rather than substantially and, in fact, coexisted for some time, as people clung to them out of fear, reverence, custom... or as a just-in-case precaution. So Jupiter was still the Father (King) whose son was ignominiously killed, and Pluto was synonymous with the Evil One in charge of the Underworld. Dreams could be visions or prophecies—as in biblical times. Seers and wizards were still consulted and feared. Miracles and magic phenomena were reported by travellers and troubadours. The old gods survived as long as people believed in them.

Their imminent Gotterdammerung was postponed, perhaps, until this story made the rounds of oral tradition in medieval Europe for five centuries before Boccaccio wrote it down in 1338 as IL FILOCOLO (The Love Worker). I translated it as part of my dissertation at Loyola University of Chicago in 1974. What you are about to read bears only a passing resemblance to the original, complex version.

It is the story of two young lovers brought together and then separated by fate, hatred, and the wilful intervention of forces opposed to the joy, freedom, and spontaneity of love. If all that evokes echoes of other famous lovers, let it be known that long before

TRISTAN and ISOLDE,
ROMEO and JULIET,
PAOLO and FRANCESCA,
there were FLORIO and BIANCOFIORE.
This is their peripatetic love story.

Chapter One

Long before the first scout returned with arrows tormenting his broken back, the horses knew that there were strange steeds around. They had been arching and buckling and neighing with dilated nostrils as if they had just finished a sweat-whipped chariot race in the Colosseum. But this was not Roma, and Consul Lellio understood his horses better than most courtiers who had followed him and his wife, Julia, on their votive pilgrimage to Santiago de Compostela. They had overcome various dangers on this long and perilous journey—brigands, marauding tribes, and battle-starved mercenaries looking for hire or for booty, the usual attackers of religious caravans. But this was no ordinary enemy. The horses flayed because they smelled the approach of more powerful and swifter animals. When the mortally wounded scout was pulled down from his horse, a look at the flared wings of the arrows confirmed his fears: Spaniards riding Arabian horses were near, maybe even surrounding them. And there was no time to turn around in this heavily wooded trail in the northern territories. Lellio knew he would soon fight for his life and that of his expecting wife.

"I should have listened to my instincts," he said to himself. But he hadn't, four months earlier.

His three close friends and officers looked at him for orders. Sesto Fulvio, noble and daring, was in charge of the younger group of strong, well-trained fighters. They were always the first line of attack. Ostazio Artifilo, leader of a group of pilgrims that had joined them along the way for company and safety in number, would come right behind Fulvio's men. Sculpizio Gaio, a dear cousin, led the gentlemen of the group, the old guard in charge of defending the caravan's women and weak pilgrims.

Lellio spoke to them. "Remember that you are followers of the new Holy Law, for which Jupiter's son suffered a cruel death to free us from Pluto's unholy hands in which our first father put us with his disobedience. To uphold his Law and save ourselves we will offer our bodies, if necessary. But we are also Romans fighting to save our families, our honour, and our civilisation. We will not die like sheep to attacking wolves. Are you ready to follow me?"

The soldiers roared their approval. Julia heard the speech and came out of the baldachin-covered wagon in which she was riding with her maidens. Obviously pregnant, beautiful with long black hair flowing over her silk garments, a silver cross resting on her florid chest, she could easily have been a model for a Madonna painting, but for the tears streaming down her cheeks. She waved her hand in distress and to attract Lellio's attention to speak. The crowd hushed in respect and affection for her.

"Before you go to your death, let me tell you what's in my heart. I fear for us, the living and the unborn. I am a woman of courage, but also a mother-to-be and as such I treasure life more than all the diamonds in King Solomon's mines. Most of you know that we have travelled for months to keep a vow made after five years of childless marriage. We tried everything: mandrake roots, moonlight incantations, ablutions and flagellation, amulets and pigeons' feet. Nothing worked until a hermit suggested praying to the martyr in Compostela. He answered our prayers. Now we are keeping our promise to Him... if we can make it through this obstacle, which I feel has been conjured up by the Evil One who thrives on discord and bloodshed. Let us not fall for this trick. Give our attackers all they want: gold, beasts, and provisions. We can buy more later. They will let us go if we do not fight them. Why shouldn't they? They won't lose any men. Our men will only lose some pride. What is that compared to a life? To many lives?" She spread her arms out as if to embrace everyone.

The people murmured their approval, then turned to Lellio already battle-armed on his horse. Lellio looked at Julia with sadness, love, and understanding. But he had a job to do, and soon. He turned to her and then to the crowd. "If the people approaching us were mere thieves, they would have come in the darkness of night to steal while we slept. They would have not sent back our scout with their signature arrows on his back. They want to scare us. They want us to know they are coming to kill us all, take our belongings, and enslave our women. I don't know why they consider us their enemy since we have never hurt anyone but to defend ourselves. And obviously, the crosses and olive branches we carry as our standards have no meaning to them. So we must fight them. May Jupiter be on our side. If he is not, *dulce et decorum est pro patria mori.*" (It is sweet and dignified to die for one's country.)

Each man beat his breast with the hilt of his sword, repeating: "*Pro Patria Mori.*"

Lellio then ordered the old gentleman Sculpizio Gaio to take Julia to the rear of the caravan and hide her there with the other women. He gave a hand signal to the other two groups not to follow until they were needed. Standing straight in his stirrups, he surveyed his knights and read that resolute ardour and readiness on their faces. He liked what he saw and smiled his approval. When he shouted, "Lance-Ho!" they fell into a wedge formation with Lellio as its spearhead. They raised their shields above their heads and advanced with slow, close-order, cadenced steps. They were ready to kill or be killed.

Chapter Two

The clanging of arms, the thumping of hooves, and the thrashing of bushes announced the arrival of the enemy hordes. Then a shower of arrows filled the sky and arched toward the Romans. But the Romans were already too close for the archers to hit the intended targets. Most arrows fell harmlessly behind them. The battle was enjoined. Lellio pushed his horse toward a huge barbarian who seemed to be in charge of the first group of attackers. When their spears missed their marks because the Romans closed in so fast, Lellio surged with his horse toward the leader and plunged his lance into his stupefied face. Sesto, galloping next to Lellio, struck another in a similar way. Soon all their lances were used and broken. The Romans pulled out their swords and continued slashing at the enemies, killing many of them. Unfortunately, the enemy kept pushing against the outnumbered Romans, forcing them to retreat even as they were fighting valiantly. Lellio moved around, reminding his men, "You're fighting to save yourselves for your parents, your children, your wives. They need you back home. Fight to return to them." His men, responding with greater ardour and vigour, began to repulse their foes.

Captain Scurmenide, one of those foes, seeing his soldiers retreat under the Roman attack, cursed at his men. "I will personally kill anyone who retreats." He then went around scolding apathetic soldiers, rearming those who had lost their weapons, and pushing with his horse those hesitating to move forward. His men counterattacked, arms resounding under the power of blows, swords broken by swords, bones crushed by shields. The sounds of the battle soon included the screams and wailing of the wounded.

Sesto and his group could no longer hold on; his already small retinue had been reduced to a handful of men. Lellio realised it was time to bring in Artifilo and his group who had been straining to get into the battle. They moved in with order and eagerness. The first enemy Artifilo went for was Scurmenide, into whose belly he plunged his lance to leave him dead on the dusty field. Artifilo's men killed many at first, but were soon decimated by the greater number of enemies. Artifilo, having lost his lance, began using a sharp axe and, fighting on the left flank, went about killing anyone who stood in his way. Lellio and Sesto were fighting on the right side of the wedge.

A brave warrior named Menaab, enraged by the slaughter enjoyed by Artifilo with his new weapon, took a bow and aimed it under the arm raised with the axe, wounding him there with a poisoned arrow. But Artifilo pulled the arrow out with his own hand, turned his horse toward Menaab—who was already set to shoot another arrow—overcame him and hit him on the head with such strength as to split it in two parts. Surrounded by many, with his horse killed under him, he stood on top of it and defended himself vigorously.

The furious foes pushed all around him, but Artifilo killed anyone who came near him. Soon there were so many bodies around him that they were piled as high as his horse. When his axe lost its cutting edge, he used it to break the bones of the fiercest fighters. A rain of arrows began to fall on Artifilo, breaking his hard helmet in many pieces, and covering his back with more arrows than his own armour. Yet no one dared to come near him. It was he who went over dead bodies, reached for his enemies, killing them while he called his friends to help him and his enemies to come to him.

Tarpelio, a nephew of the king, heard him and made his way among the knights to wound him in the chest with a big lance. Artifilo, already weakened by the loss of blood, fell on the ground, where he was promptly killed by Tarpelio's friends.

When Lellio, who had been watching Artifilo, saw him fall, he ran over there, to help Artifilo's friends fighting angrily to avenge their captain's death. He fought next to them for a while, but when he spotted Sesto, wounded in several places, fighting on almost alone, he realised that he himself was in trouble. So he ordered Sesto and his few men to pull back and join Sculpizio Gaio's group—their last resort.

They continued to fight with as much if not more vigour than before. In this, they were aided by the sheer number of enemies crowded in such a small space that one's sword often impeded the other's sword because of the close quarters. In fact, Sesto and Sculpizio, now fighting ahead of the others with their few knights, made the enemy retreat into nearby fields untouched by the battle.

At that point, their leader, King Felix, who had come down from the mountain with a fresh company of soldiers, surrounded the tired fighters and sent a storm of arrows and lances at the diminishing group of Romans with a deadly canopy. They gathered in a circle so small that those who were slain by the oncoming arrows, against which there was no defence, remained straight up, their bodies supported by the surviving, fighting companions. But the Romans were not giving up their struggle.

Sculpizio was the first one who left the encircled group. He ran toward the king and struck him so vigorously on the helmet that the king fell down from his horse, stunned. But with the help of his people, the king quickly recovered. Lellio and Sesto resumed the battle, carving great spaces around them with their swords. Nevertheless, Sesto was soon surrounded by many enemies. When his horse was killed under him, he fell in the middle of the field and, wound-weakened as he was, he was quickly killed.

Seeing his friend die, Lellio ran over to a warrior who was about to strip Sesto of his armour and struck him with his sword hard enough to fling the man's left arm on the ground along with the shield. The man himself fell dead upon Sesto.

The king, enraged to see Lellio fight so valiantly although he had lost most of his weapons, came as close as possible to him, threw his lance at his throat with such force that it knocked Lellio off his horse and onto the ground, dead. Sculpizio immediately ran to kill the king with his sword, and he would have succeeded if a knight named Favenzio had not placed himself in the path of the blow. Sculpizio's sword fell on his shining helmet, cut through it, and cleaved him almost to his teeth. But when Sculpizio tried to pull out the sword for a second blow, he could not retrieve it. While still trying, he was struck from behind by the king's men and finally slain. One by one the Romans died after fighting with their last spurt of energy and their last weapon. But they were outnumbered by hordes of attackers. Not one of Lellio's retinue survived the attack.

King Felix ordered his men to make camp near the battlefield for the night. They did and then, with the king's permission, they began to pillage the remains of the caravan, taking any arms, riches, and garments they could find. They did so in a very short time. Meanwhile the king went around surveying the bloodied battlefield and comforting the wounded. That night many could not sleep because of the painful cries of the dying soldiers. One of them was Julia.

Chapter Three

Julia heard the anguished cries of the wounded and ran outside the shepherd hut to find out what had happened. Her ladies-in-waiting tried to hold her back, but she was determined to know. When she saw the carnage before her, she knew. But she still could not believe.

"Where are our men? Where is my Lellio? What happened to everybody? Who did this?" Nobody dared answer the obvious. She looked around. Her face hardened by the enormity of the tragedy, her eyes dilated to take in the horrendous mounds of bodies rigid in grotesque positions, her ears tuning in to the wailing of waning agonies, she could barely mumble: "Lellio, Lellio. Where are you?"

The only other sounds were the noises of the pillagers. And then she saw them. Inchoate faces. Incoherent clothes. Incomprehensible language. Unusual arms and lurid insignia. And unrecognisable bodies everywhere. Her women tried to bring her back to her hut and to her sanity.

She screamed at them, "Let me go. It is not right that such a hero should be left to rot in a field, away from his home, without being mourned and cried over.

The fates denied him the tears of his father, his relatives, and the Roman people. Do you dare deny him even the tears of his wife?"

She pushed her women away, put her hands in her blonde hair and began to pull them furiously out of order and style. She rendered her garments as she walked toward the carnage, pushing away limbs, bodies and faces, looking for Lellio. It was almost impossible to recognise friends from foes until she spotted Lellio's heralded armour. She knelt by him and cuddled his face on her lap, crying bitterly and swooning over him. After a while she raised herself and began to beat herself with bloodied hands and to scratch her cheeks. Soon she had hurt herself so much that her beautiful face looked as bloodied as the bodies on that field. And she did not mind drenching her lips in Lellio's wounds, which she kissed with bitter tears and embraced tightly, shaking uncontrollably.

"Why didn't you listen to me? Where have you abandoned me? Among people with customs so different from ours that I do not know any of them? I wish Jupiter would have let them treat me as cruelly as they did you. We would be together now. But, no, you could not listen to a woman's advice when you went against Jupiter's will to fulfil yours. If He had wanted us to have children, He would have given us that happiness without any extravagant vow. Now, all I want is to die like my ancestor Cornelia Julia, and be with my

Lellio."

And she tried to pierce herself with broken lances, which her women promptly took away. She called to the pillagers to kill her. They ignored her as they would a crazy person. Julia remained prostrate over her husband's body crying loudly, wailing into the night along with her women.

Somehow their wailing reached the ears of King Felix who himself could not help but think about the horrendous battle and its cost in human lives. As the crying did not abate, the unnerved king called in his attendant knight, Ascaleon, and told him to find the source of that crying. Ascaleon and his men set out into the night with torches and by just following the unceasing wailing they reached Julia.

Chapter Four

Julia looked at the face and attire of the men who approached her and knew they were the enemy. She rose to face Ascaleon, whose armour singled him out as a leader, wiped her tears with a handkerchief, and spoke to him with dignity, even as she sobbed.

"Today you mercilessly killed Lellio, my comfort and hope. Now show some mercy and kill me so that I may join him in the shadows of his new world. If you can't, let me have your sword and allow me to die like a Roman lady, not like a slave."

Ascaleon, moved by the bloodied face of Julia and her noble countenance, shook his head. "My lady, I will not do either because I do not believe in killing. In fact, today I did not participate in that slaughter. But your death will in no way bring back your husband, and neither will your tears. In time, by living, you may still regain the comfort you have lost. But now you and your companions should come with me to the king's pavilions, where you will be much safer. There are beasts in these woods and unscrupulous men in our army who would gladly prey on your bodies. You deserve a better fate than that. And I swear by the gods

I worship, my king will honour you in the way you are accustomed to as a noble lady."

Julia, visibly touched by the words of Ascaleon, bowed to him in gratitude. "By the way you speak my language and by your manners, you captured my doleful soul and I cannot refuse your offer. So I put myself and our honour in your hands as if we were your sisters." She barely finished her words when she fainted from weakness or relief.

Ascaleon lifted her promptly by the arms and, aided by her companions, walked her gingerly to the king's pavilion and entered it. When she saw the king, she knelt before him and cried softly.

"High lord, since I am your prisoner, give me the death that your knight denied me. I deserve it because of my fierce intentions of revenge for what your people did to my husband."

The king did not allow Julia to lie prone before him, but raised her with his own hands and made her sit before him as he spoke to her.

"Young lady, your tears could evoke pity from a marble statue. But I understand that your anger more than reason speaks for you, so I shall neither grant you death nor believe your emotional words. But tell me, who are you? Where are you coming from and where are you going to?"

"I am the unfortunate wife of Lellio, the Roman consul you slew today with your own hands. We were going to the Holy Shrine in your kingdom as a thanksgiving for the gift of my pregnancy."

The king turned livid with stupor. "Then you were not among those who attacked and burned my beloved city of Marmorina?"

"No, sir," replied Julia. "But as we went through it, we admired its great beauty."

The king, visibly shaken by her words, heaved deep breaths as he spoke to her.

"Young lady, it is almost impossible to escape the fickleness of fate. We were told in a dream—or was it a vision—? the very opposite of what you just told us, and that prompted us to do something that cannot be reversed and for which I am very sorry. We both sustained great losses because of my rash furore and someone's treachery. Your husband, my nephew and many knights are out there lifeless. But in retribution for the pain I have caused you, I am offering some choices: you can stay here as long as you wish as my guest. In time, if you decide to have another husband, I will gladly give you the one you like the most among my noblest knights. If you want to remain faithful to your dead husband, I will honour you as a dear relative in the company of my wife. If you want to leave after giving birth, I will have you royally escorted to any place of your choice. I promise you all this on my father's soul."

Realising that in her condition in a strange land and without escort she would come to a bad end, Julia accepted his protection. "My lord, my life and my death are in your hands. I will never deviate from what pleases you. I only ask that Lellio and his knights be given a proper burial."

The king ordered that her wish be carried out and that she and her companions be treated with honour in one of the pavilions, under the trusted watch of Ascaleon. The bodies were burned on a pyre and the ashes buried respectfully. And it was done. In the morning, the king and his retinue (along with Julia) started out toward Seville, the ancient city in the Hesperian kingdom. When they arrived there, the king brought Julia to meet his wife, who was also expecting a baby. He commanded that she be held as a dear companion and left her with the queen.

Julia spent many a day sighing and crying to the point when the queen told her that such behaviour would be hurtful to her and most of all to the baby growing in her womb. Julia was touched by the sincerity and wisdom of her words and resigned herself to her fate more graciously. In fact, she began making exquisite silken tapestries for the queen. Her work and her talents endeared her (and her companions) to the queen even more. They became so close to each other that they even went into labour at the same time, but with opposite results. The queen gave birth to a boy, thus assuring the king of an heir to his throne and giving the town a reason for enjoying an entire week of festivities. Julia, on the other hand, gave birth to a beautiful girl, but died in the process. Before she expired, she thanked God for fulfilling her two wishes—a progeny and death—and commended her daughter to the caring hands of Gloritia (her trusted maid). The death of Julia affected Gloritia deeply, as she cried out while holding the baby in her arms, "Oh daughter of tears and anguish, before your birth you caused the death of your father and at birth you killed your mother. It is clear that your birth displeases Jupiter and puts a bitter weight on me to become a mother, I who know not any man."

And she continued to wail, so long and loud together with the other women that the queen heard the commotion. Surprised that at a time for rejoicing some people were crying like mourners, she sent a servant to inquire about the cause of such behaviour. The servant came back quickly with the news of Julia's death and the birth of her daughter. The queen's tears of joy soon turned to tears of sadness as she really had grown fond of Julia. She arranged for Julia to be honourably buried on the next day; then she took the pretty baby in her arms, kissed her many times while crying and said, "Since it has pleased your mother to be no longer with us, you will remain in her place as a dear daughter. You shall be a dear friend of my son and always a relative." Many times in the future, the queen would cry over those prophetic words.

Meanwhile, the king ordered that Julia's cleansed

body be wrapped in royal vestments and placed in a marbled tomb, as befitting so noble a lady, and that the following verse be etched on her grave:

> *Having been cut by Atropos' shears*
> *Lady Julia Topazia of Rome lies here.*
> *Born from Caesar's high blood and race,*
> *she was beautiful, fair, and full of grace.*
> *At childbirth she left us in manner undue*
> *for which our hearts will not cease to rue*
> *and blame her High God (to us but unknown)*
> *for his great misdeed that left her undone.*

A few days later, the king decided it was time to see his son and the Roman girl born on the same day. Once he had them both in his arms, he looked at them for a long time admiring their beauty and strange resemblance. He then announced to the group that because they were born like flowers on the first day of spring, the boy would be named FLORIO and the girl BIANCOFIORE. He then returned the babies to the queen, admonishing her to take good care of Florio, but also to hold Biancofiore very dearly because she had looks that in beauty would surpass any woman and because he wanted to keep her forever in place of Julia. After that, highly pleased to have such a handsome heir and such a beautiful companion, he left the queen's chambers.

The queen entrusted the babies to a wet-nurse who took care of them until they were weaned. The king often fussed over them and always had them dressed like royalty. Biancofiore, who grew more beautiful every day, was almost as dear to him as Florio. When they reached the age of six, he summoned two wise men, Racheio and Ascaleon, both expert tutors, and commissioned them to teach the two children to read and write efficiently. He then told Ascaleon to teach them any and all customs becoming a gentleman and gentlewoman, because he had fixed his greatest hopes on them as his last mission. The first book that old Ascaleon taught them to read was Ovid's *Ars Amatoria*, *The Art of Love Making*, in which the poet shows how the fires of Venus must be lit in cold hearts. If he only knew how well his pupils would follow Ovid's teachings.

Chapter Five

Somewhere in the skies above Mount Olympus, the goddess Venus heard her name mentioned often and endearingly by Florio and Biancofiore as they were reading the book of love. Pleased as she was by their diligence, she was not content that their learning should be only a reading exercise. So she flew onto the high mountain of Cytherea where her son, Cupid, was tempering new arrows in holy waters. She quickly ordered him to stop his arrow-making and fly down to Spain to appear to the children under the guise of King Felix. His mission would be to infuse the children with his fire and inflame one another in such a way that Love would be in their hearts forever. Cupid obeyed his mother and entered the children's playroom after assuming the appearance of the king. As such, he picked up Florio first, brought him to his chest and kissed him as the king would have, but with a twist. He infused in his heart a desire, which Florio innocently reinforced by gazing with delight into the shining eyes of Biancofiore. He did the same with Biancofiore with similar results before he returned to his work.

From that moment, the children began to look at

each other and to wonder silently and timorously, not understanding what had happened, but not wanting to leave the other, no matter what. The secret potion of Cupid was quickly working in their hearts.

Florio was the first one to close the book and speak. "What has happened just now that makes me like you so much? I did not feel this way before. Now... I can't take my eyes off of you. You are so beautiful."

"I do not know," answered Biancofiore. "I feel the same way about you. Maybe these verses have somehow inflamed our minds as they did to the people in the book."

"It must be," admitted Florio, "because suddenly I like you more than anything in the world."

While they were talking with their books closed, their teacher Racheio walked in on them. "Is this something new that I see? Studying with closed books?"

The children turned red in their faces and quickly opened their books, but whereas before they could read fluently on any given page, they now stammered and stumbled, their attention being more on each other than on the books. Their teacher took notice of that and decided to check on them more closely. He began to hide behind draperies and columns while they were studying. He quickly discovered that as soon as he left the room, they would give each other simple kisses, but no more. Racheio did not need further evidence to realise that the fire of Venus had so inflamed them that it would take a long time for the coldness of Diana, goddess of chastity, to cool them off. Fearing to lose his sinecure job, he confided in Ascaleon and asked for his advice.

Ascaleon decided that they should tell the king immediately before something bad happened for which they could be blamed. They did, after much trepidation.

King Felix did not like what he heard. He told the tutors to keep vigilant and to chastise the children as needed until he himself came up with some drastic remedy. But for that he needed time and absolute quiet to think. So he dismissed everyone from his quarters and began to walk and to talk and to gesticulate in erratic ways. But he was the king. Nobody would approach him or dissuade him. Nobody, that is, but the queen who happened to be passing through that room, when she asked him for the cause of his puzzling behaviour — maybe she could help him with some advice or comfort.

The king was relieved to tell her. "What Fortune gives you with the right hand, she often takes away with the left hand. She gave us riches, victory, and Florio. Now she's already depriving us of him in a vile way by making him so inflamed with Biancofiore that he sees no farther than her beauty, according to their teachers. I do not mind that he loves, but I grieve that the one he loves is not equal to his nobility. If she were of royal blood, we would join them promptly in matrimony. But to fall in love with a Roman plebeian nourished as a servant in our home? A boy who will administer our kingdoms lost to a little girl? But what can I do? If I try to separate them by force, he might become more inflamed with her and leave us for good. And if I stay silent, his fire within will grow hotter every hour, and we will never be able to separate him from her."

The queen was saddened by those words, but not as depressed as the king. She had an idea. "You are right, my dear," she said. "But I can see why he can fall in love with such a beautiful, young, and likeable girl. And if this love goes on, our son will be lost alive, given the low condition of Biancofiore. But we must act now. Fresh scars can be healed more easily than old ones. So, the best solution is to separate them now, and this is how we'll do it. Florio, already schooled in holy studies, needs to get into more abstract subjects, and the best school for that is in Montorio, where reigns our relative Duke Ferramonte. We send Florio there to study for a while. Away from her, he will soon forget her. At that time, we can give him a spouse of royal blood, and your troubles are over. So chase out your melancholy and act on this plan without hesitation."

The king liked the queen's advice and promised to heed it at once. Didn't he know that nothing is more desired than what is very difficult if not impossible to get? Maybe not, since as a king he could get everything. Or could he?

Chapter Six

The next day he summoned Florio to his vast library and sat him on a small stool across from his reading table, which he had loaded with books and scrolls. He then spoke to him paternally. "My handsome son, dear to me above all things, listen patiently to my words and obey my wishes. Since the gods have blessed me with such a healthy and bright heir to take over our occidental kingdoms, I thought that you might become a better leader if you study the scientific arts and master the principles of Pythagoras, as did King Solomon, the wisest of monarchs. For that purpose, you need not go to Athens since in nearby Montorio those sciences are taught in superb manner under the governance of our dear relative, Duke Ferramonte. You could take whichever companion you like and leave immediately for this short trip. Of course, we would visit you often without disturbing your studies. What do you think?"

Florio was very much perturbed by his father's wishes, which ran contrary to his desire. He stood there staring at the floor for a long time, silent and brooding. He finally answered him. "Father, I don't understand why you want to separate me from you at such a young age and in such a hurry. And what makes you think that I would study more and better away from you? Actually, I would worry constantly about your health and your safety, as one does for the ones he loves. And what if the gods call you to their realms while I am away? With such thoughts, could I really concentrate on my studies? If anything, wouldn't it be better if you bring those great teachers here where I could learn more and better in your presence?"

The king knew the reason behind Florio's reply. But he was not about to give in.

"The reality of death should not dissuade us from doing what we must do. Weak fathers spoil their children because they love them too much. That will not happen here. For your benefit I will steel myself to separate you from me for a while. Indeed, you should appreciate this since your destiny demands more preparation than ease. Then too it is becoming for young men to get a greater education by learning the customs and languages of other people. The respect of the world is not attained without hardship. Besides, going to Montorio will not be going away from me. It is still our kingdom. Therefore go, study hard, and in a short time you can return to me, an educated youth with no more need to study."

Incapable to hold back the truth, Florio finally confessed it to his father. "Father, I would go anywhere to please you. But to what end? What would I look for if what I want is right here? The truth is that in our royal house lives the one I love above all things: Biancofiore, the ultimate goal of my desire. Her beautiful face, which shines even more than a morning star, is what I wish to study. I will die away from her. Still, you can send me anywhere you want *if* you allow her to go with me. Then no hardship will be too great for me. If you love me and want my happiness, grant my wish, dear Father."

Angry as he was, the king did not show it. In fact, he leaned closer to Florio, as if to confide a secret. "I would, but right now the queen suffers from a strange depression that only the presence of Biancofiore at her bedside can alleviate. But as soon as the queen recovers, Biancofiore will come to you. You have my word on that."

Florio had no reason to disbelieve him. "In that case, I will obey your wish, Father."

"Be ready to leave tomorrow, then," said the king curtly and left the room.

As he did, he did not notice Biancofiore moving around a large tapestry to enter the library. She ran tearfully into Florio's arms. He held her for a while until she stopped crying.

"How could you?" she lashed out at him. "How could you promise him that? Couldn't you see that he was doing it only so you would consent to leave without embarrassing him? Away from me, he hopes you will forget me. He knows what he is doing, even if you don't.

But this I can promise you: if I am not sent to you, I will still come. I'll find a way, sooner or later."

"And so will I," affirmed Florio. "I will keep my word so people can't say I want to do everything in my way. If he breaks his promise to send you, I will have a legitimate reason for coming back."

"They will certainly treat me like a slave when you are gone. Maybe even kill me, if I don't kill myself first. And you have already done that to my heart."

"What? Anyone who touches you will die by my hands. I swear it." He walked around to find the words that would justify him. "What? Be disrespectful with my father?" He turned around again and did not see her nodding vigorously. "If you tell me not to go there, I won't, even if he kills me."

She shook her head repeatedly.

"Forget you? Impossible. No woman will ever own my soul but you."

Biancofiore was clearly touched by the forceful sincerity of his words. She pulled a ring from her dress pocket and put it in Florio's right hand.

"This ring, given by Hannibal's brother to Scipio the African, was passed down the generations to my mother, who gave it to Gloritia for me. It has magic powers. If I am in danger, it will become cloudy. When it does, come to me as quickly as possible. So look at it often, at the very least to remember me. Most of all, if your father does not keep his promise, you keep yours:

return to your Biancofiore before it's too late."

They kissed tenderly, albeit confusedly, as young lovers do at their first encounters. They mixed their kisses with tears, promises, and sighs before they said goodbye and went to their chambers. Neither one slept much that night. The ship of their future was navigating toward very troubled waters… and they were not at the helm.

Chapter Seven

Florio left Marmorina the next day, but not alone. With him went many young knights whose only goal in life was to have fun and to find different ways to do so. On the way to Montorio they released falcons to chase and capture doves and quails; they let their dogs hunt down deer and boars; and they drank and sang merrily to entertain themselves on the short trip to their destination.

All Florio did was to look back at his father's palace and try to see if Biancofiore was watching him from the highest tower's parapet. He did not see her, but she was watching him until he disappeared into the forest. She then went downstairs to cry with and be consoled by Gloritia. She was inconsolable, and so was Florio.

The duke, Ferramonte, met him at the city gates with a cortege of knights and ladies dressed in splendid clothes, riding horses covered with gold-stitched saddles and reins, and entertained by musicians playing lively songs and lovely girls dancing in veils and silk sashes. It was a day of feasting and rejoicing as if a general had returned triumphantly from a glamorous battle. The feasting continued for three days because the duke wanted to impress on his young relative how much he enjoyed his arrival there.

Florio pretended to enjoy himself, but he was actually heavy-hearted for having left Biancofiore behind. Eventually, his feelings became known to all around him. Although there was much merriment most of the time, he spent his days thinking about and talking about Biancofiore. So much so that soon he neglected his studies, his eating, and even his personal appearance—something he had never done before. When he could not sleep at night, he often rode all the way to his father's gates, on the improbable chance that he might meet Biancofiore. He never did. He began to lose weight and good colouring as well as strength and stamina.

His tutor Ascaleon tried to discipline him, counsel him, cheer him up, but to no avail. The pretty girls of Montorio made obvious their adulation for Florio's good looks, but he was not impressed. In fact, their reactions made him suspect that handsome men in Marmorina were courting Biancofiore just like that. As the days and the months passed, Florio began to worry more and more about Biancofiore. He looked at the magic ring, but he saw no sign of trouble or danger. Maybe the ring wasn't magic after all. He became more depressed and more solitary. Not long after, he abandoned his studies completely. At that point,

Ascaleon sent word to the king about Florio's behaviour and deterioration, and his obsession for Biancofiore at the expense of his mental, physical, and emotional health. Infuriated by the news, the king consulted with the queen. Something had to be done to save Florio from himself or rather from the influence of that wench Biancofiore.

Chapter Eight

The queen seemed both infuriated and exultant when the king asked for her advice, and she gave it to him. Indeed, she had waited for this opportunity for fifteen years, the age of the children, and now she could vent her anger with impunity.

"Ah, it's the gods' payback time. What business did you have killing all those Roman pilgrims? But since you had done that, why did you spare the life of that one woman who was begging for death? Either those deaths or her survival displeased the gods enough to kindle this Biancofiore fire in your house. Mark my word: as long as Biancofiore is alive, Florio will never forget her. Indeed, we will lose our son to her. So let us think how she must die."

"And rather today than tomorrow," shot back the king.

"Good. But we need a legitimate reason to let her die quickly without being blamed for it. Otherwise Florio might kill himself or leave us forever. We must find a way that will exonerate us from her death."

The queen paced around the room, talking to herself, gesticulating, and waving her hands to discard some poor choices, until she stopped and pointed her finger at her husband.

"Your birthday is coming next week, right?"

The king nodded. "Yes."

"And all the barons will come to your banquet."

Again, the king nodded.

"At that time, you announce your favourite dish—what is that, chicken?"

"Peacock, not chicken."

"Peacock. Right. If I remember well, you order the chief steward, Seneschal Massamutino, to bring it out. But this time you designate Biancofiore to do the honours and liven up the feast with her beauty. And you know, all those knights lust after her."

The king asserted his agreement, but his obvious bewilderment told that he still did not understand.

The queen explained icily, "What they don't know is what I and the seneschal have planned for their entertainment." And she whispered in his ear their diabolical plan.

At one point the king exclaimed in horror. "Argo?"

"Argo. Or would you rather try it on a guest? You always feed that mongrel, anyway. As soon as the dog dies, every guest will agree she deserves the stake."

The king first agreed with her plan, then he stopped, his face brooding with suspicion.

"But how do you know the seneschal will go along with this?"

"My maids bring me all the court gossip. He hates Biancofiore because she constantly refuses his *advances and* makes fun of him." A sinister smile completed her reply.

The king applauded again. "I will talk to him immediately. And her beauty will not sway me from what must be done to save our son and our kingdom."

"You are finally talking like the king I married sixteen years ago. Welcome to the court, sire."

Chapter Nine

The king left the queen and immediately sent for his chief steward, the seneschal Massamutino—an evil and fierce man in looks and disposition.

When the seneschal came, the king signalled to him to shut the door and come closer. The seneschal obeyed, as he was wont to do, and leaned near the king to hear him whisper.

"You know that any secret of mine was never kept from your ears or told to anyone else. But this is the greatest of all. I must deviate from the righteous path to meet a danger greater than the sin I will commit. Through no fault of mine, the fates have led me to this fork in the road: I either let Biancofiore die unjustly *or* lose my son Florio ignominiously to her. Beautiful as she is, she is a Roman commoner, and as such not suited to be the future queen of Spain. But he is so in love with her that, if I have her killed for no just reason, he will have no other wife, our throne will have no heir, and our House will have no honour. So, here is what we will do."

He motioned to the seneschal to come even closer and whispered his plan into his ear.

The seneschal listened intently, nodding at every detail relayed, his facial expression and dilating eyes clearly savouring the treacheries being planned. He was completely elated to be part of the plot against Biancofiore.

When the king had relayed to him the entire queen's plan, the seneschal left as he had come, furtively through a side door, rubbing his hands with great satisfaction.

Biancofiore would pay for her arrogant refusal of his proffers.

Chapter Ten

The king's birthday celebration would take place in the Royal Hall, a place of beauty, art, and history. Marble columns of various colours supported its high vaults artistically decorated with gold plates, and windows divided by small crystal columns allowed light to enter the room in spectral arrays. The windows were made with Indian elephant bones, all adorned with subtle intaglios on the doors, representing ancient stories—the destruction of Thebes; the pyres of Jocasta's sons; the two destructions of Troy; the victories of Alexander; the battle of Pharsalus between Caesar and Pompey; and, above all those, the painting of Jupiter served by Dionysius. Tables bedecked with gold and silver tableware, musicians playing every instrument in music, evoked praise and wonder from every guest invited to the royal celebration.

When it was time to eat, the guests sat at their designated place in order of importance. The king was flanked by six of his highest barons sitting with him, three on each side. On his right were seated Parmenion, from the royal house of Thrace; Ascaleon, the noble and old knight; Messaallino, son of the king of Granada. To his left were, Ferramonte, duke of Montorio (who had left Florio alone to come to the feast); Sara, a fierce lord from the Barca mountains; and Menedon, a descendant of Jarbas, king of the Gaetulians. All other nobles were seated at lower tables, served by very noble youths.

Biancofiore, seated next to the queen, wore a purple chamois dress. Her blonde hair bridled in a tress rolled around her head, and a small crown shining with precious stones completed her beautiful attire.

After most of the meat had been consumed, it was time to bring in the much-heralded "Peacock". Seneschal Massamutino came before the queen, bowed deeply, and spoke.

"Your Majesty, to enhance the celebration of our king's birthday, we have prepared a special peacock, which we want to present before the king and his barons to offer their traditional pledges, which will make this feast even greater. Thus, it is proper that such a bird be brought to the royal table by a very noble and beautiful maiden. That said, there is none here or in the city who can compare to Biancofiore in any way. Therefore, allow her to come forth with us to bring the peacock out at this very moment."

The queen appeared to be nervous and hesitant to grant such a proper request for some reason. The people around began to comment on her delayed silence. The king looked at her sternly. The queen understood and relinquished any hesitation or scruple harboured at the moment. She gave permission to Biancofiore and urged her on. "Go on, Biancofiore, but you must exact the boastful pledges from all barons, before you place the peacock before the king and come back here, keeping in mind the pledge of every baron."

Biancofiore did exactly as she had been told. She brought the plate in and approached the king's table, after making the deepest reverence to the king and bowing kindly to the barons. Then she spoke.

"As the gods have been kind enough to give me this honour over so many other pretty ladies, I bring to your royal presence Juno's bird, which, because of Her, deserves this respect. Anyone who makes a boastful pledge in Juno's honour must fulfil it in earnest as required by your time-honoured tradition. So, if you please, we will begin with you, dear lord king, because you are the most worthy, most senior, and most wise of the people here." And she held the peacock before him.

The king waited until there was complete silence before he spoke. "Upon the divinity of the great Jupiter and any other god in His kingdom, upon my great ancestor Atlantis, upon the soul of my father, if I am allowed to live long enough to see the day, I pledge to marry you to one of the greatest barons of my kingdom. I so swear for the love of this peacock."

In her mind, Biancofiore answered, *There is no greater baron in this world than Florio. So I can live with that without any sorrow or reservation.* She thanked the king with subdued voice and moved on to the first baron, Parmenion.

He pledged, "On the day of your wedding, my noblest companions and I, dressed in very elegant clothes, will proudly ride to the right of you and your horse with all due reverence and honour, until you are welcomed into your new house and have dismounted from your horse."

"Why then," answered Biancofiore. "I will be able to boast about my escort more than Juno." Next, she asked Ascaleon, "Dear master, what do you pledge on this bird?"

Ascaleon answered, "Beautiful young woman, although I am old and trembling, I can promise you this: on your wedding day, I will fight with sharp swords anyone who wishes to challenge me. Moreover, I will remove his sword from his hands without hurting him or myself, and I will hand it to you bloodless."

The king mused, "Anyone who can make good on such a boast will be a winner."

Biancofiore went forward to Messaallino, who, obviously smitten by her beauty, said, "Gracious maiden, for the love of you on the day you will sit at the table of the new groom, I will present you with ten plants of dates from my land, with a gold coin attached to each root."

She then presented the peacock to Duke Ferramonte, who pledged, "On your wedding day, I will fill your cup with my own hands whenever you like it and for as long as the feast lasts."

Biancofiore smiled coyly. "Of such a server even Jupiter, much less I, would be proud."

Lord Sara was ready when she came to him. "On your wedding day I will personally bring to you a glorious crown heavy with gold and precious stones."

Menedon quickly vowed, "On your wedding day, my companion lancers will exalt you by jousting and fighting throughout the entire celebration."

As this was the last pledge, Biancofiore placed the peacock before the king and spoke to him and all the barons. "I pray the gods that since my capacity to give due thanks for the promised gifts is limited, may they compensate all of you with good fortune and especially you, my dear king and singular benefactor."

She then sat demurely next to the queen, who praised her for her demeanour.

It was now time to serve the peacock. A noble young squire named Salpadin, who on that day was the designated carver, cut the peacock in half and threw some offal pieces to Argo, the king's dog. Argo grabbed one piece and ate it quickly. In no time at all, the dog became sick and began to swell as tumescence enlarged his belly and spread to his head. The dog howled, cried, and rolled on the ground while his whole body ballooned into deformity to the point that its bones could not contain it. Argo exploded and died. At the sight of the dismembered dog, the great hall became silent, save for hushed whispers. Salpadin wanted to taste the peacock, but the king stopped him.

"Do not! I'm afraid we have been betrayed by some wicked people. But just to make sure Argo did not die from something eaten before, throw a piece to another dog."

Salpadin threw a larger piece to a bigger dog, which no sooner had eaten it that it rolled in a similar way as Argo and died the same death.

The king became very enraged at the sight. "Who wants to shorten my life with poison?" he shouted. He pushed the table and overturned it. His anger was as visible as the fear on the faces of his guests. "Guards, seize Biancofiore, the seneschal, and Salpadin, and throw them in the dungeon. One of them tried to poison me and my barons. Away with them."

Biancofiore was taken to a solitary cell, away from the crowd, which seemed divided on her innocence or guilt. But no one was allowed to talk to her, and vice versa. Her screams of innocence were ignored and soon she was locked in a dark dungeon. Numb with fear, incredulity, and shock, she felt alone, as she had never felt before. She had no way to tell Florio or ask for his help. She could only weep in her solitude.

Chapter Eleven

The seneschal and Salpadin, on the other hand, were questioned immediately by the chief of justice, who released them promptly after hearing and accepting their alibis. They had never touched the peacock. Biancofiore alone had carried it from the kitchen to the hall. The king believed them and would not prosecute them. But Biancofiore was another story.

That same afternoon the king summoned a council of many people, including the six barons who had been with him that morning. Once seated in his assembly hall, he came immediately to the point.

"I have ordered you here to consider the fate of Biancofiore, since she is the only one who could have possibly wanted my death. Why? I don't know. But consider what I have done for her: I raised her from serfdom to freedom. I dressed her in royal vestments. I tutored her in science along with my son. I gave her the company of my wife in the belief that she was not an enemy, but a dear daughter. And I was ready to have her married off highly as her age and upbringing required. For all this what did I get? I cuddled a snake on my breast and I was almost bitten by it. She must be punished harshly so that no other woman will ever undertake such a deception.

"But I don't want to act impetuously, since she has conquered the hearts of many people with her beauty and false pleasantness. So, before I proceed, I want your loyal advice quickly, if you have any esteem for my crown and my life as members of this court."

After the king had spoken, everyone was silent for a long time. The duke and Ascaleon would have answered quite willingly because they suspected who had planned and executed that poisoning. But since they knew the will of the king, each remained silent, fearing to displease him. And so were the other counsellors.

The only one who spoke was Massamutino, the king's accomplice who had injected all those venomous juices into the peacock. And what did he say?

"The crime committed by Biancofiore is so evident that it cannot be covered up in any way. This in spite of all the honours you bestowed upon her. Therefore, she deserves the maximum penalty. Even if she had only *thought* of such a crime she would deserve to die. Since she planned to destroy your life with the fiery power of poison, let her life be destroyed by the fiery power of the stake. Listen, I love her very much for her beauty, yet in matters of justice, neither love, nor pity, nor friendship must make us deviate from the right path. But you are the king. You are wiser than I am. This is just my humble opinion."

Again, no one rose to defend Biancofiore or to even suggest that being isolated in the dungeon, she could not defend herself or prove her innocence. Obviously, everyone realised now that the king allowed those things to be done with his consent; therefore, everyone was silent to not displease the king. Their life could depend on it.

Encouraged by the silence of the council, the king announced his decision.

"Then, lords, in my opinion it seems that you advise that Biancofiore must die by fire, and indeed, I was myself of that opinion. Therefore, I call on the judges here present to pass their judicial sentence. It would be eminently illegal to let her die without it otherwise. On the other hand, I do not want to cause too much delay in carrying it out because justice delayed is often obstructed by pity and even denied."

The judges were trembling with fear, but they confabulated among themselves to decide what to do. At last, their oldest member spoke.

"Lord, the laws forbid us from issuing a capital sentence on a solemn day, such as today. But we will prepare the case properly and on the new day we will issue a verdict and put it into execution without failure."

Obviously annoyed by the legal obstacle, the king replied, "Since the law forbids it today, let this be done tomorrow morning early and without delay." And having said that, he left the council in haste.

The duke and Ascaleon also left the room and

departed immediately for Montorio where they arrived before sunset only to find Florio awaiting them alone.

When asked how the birthday feast had gone, the duke told him all the good things that had happened that day in spite of his absence. He made no mention of Biancofiore's ordeal or arrest. Having said that, they all went to bed.

All, but Florio. He could not sleep well, and when he did, he had a wondrous dream in which the goddess Venus warned him that Biancofiore was in danger. She then proceeded to show him visually what had happened to Biancofiore at the banquet and where she was being held. She then gave him specific orders.

"You must go to Marmorina and rescue her. Take a good horse and full armour, and wield this sword made by Vulcan. Go to the square where Biancofiore will be led to her death and tell the people of her innocence. Then confront any knight who might say otherwise. It won't be easy, but you will come through. After the fight, take Biancofiore back to your father and entrust her to his care. Do not question the will of the gods and do not identify yourself to anyone. Go and do this, no matter what Ascaleon might say to you. We are watching over both of you."

When Florio woke up, he found a sword in his hand. As he looked at it, marvelling at its beautiful design and sharpness, he glanced at the ring on his finger: it was clouded, almost opaque. He then knew that the dream had not been a nightmare.

Chapter Twelve

It was still night-time when Florio arrived at Ascaleon's house and knocked on the door several times before it was opened by Ascaleon himself.

"What are you doing here at this hour, and why did you come alone?" asked Ascaleon, utterly flummoxed by the unceremonious visit.

"I need full armour and a war horse immediately and in complete secrecy. You are the only one who can do this for me in this town." Florio spoke firmly, while hiding the magic sword behind him.

Ascaleon was not sure what to make of that demand. So he tried to humour Florio. "But if you tell me what has turned a student of Ovid into a disciple of Mars, maybe I can help you achieve your goal without jeopardising your life."

Florio was undeterred. "You know what happened yesterday, yet you told me nothing. But in a dream, Venus showed me the entire episode. Now with this sword" —and he showed it to him— "which she gave me, I will rescue Biancofiore or die rather than live without her."

Ascaleon saw an opening there. "Dear child, a

dream? You believe in a bad dream caused by too much or not enough eating? And you'd fight for whom? A girl of low class, daughter of a queen's maid, who was raised with you to keep you company, not to become a queen. And even if you went ahead with this madness, it would only make your father hate her more. Leave her to her fate. She did it. She deserves it."

Florio glared at him inches from his face. "And what prompts you now to call Biancofiore a maid's daughter when you've told me so many times that her father was a Roman nobleman? And didn't you teach me that nobility comes not from one's bloodline, but from the good deeds of a virtuous mind? And my father? He never sent me Biancofiore as he had promised. What kind of father is that? I would kill him or anyone else to free Biancofiore."

He stopped, almost in shock by what he had said.

"Look, I have the vision, the sword, and the ring to verify the truth. And in case you still doubt my words, your peacock pledge was to disarm any swordsman without hurting him or yourself in the process. Now will you help me deliver Biancofiore from the fire? Because if you can't or won't, I will go at it alone."

Ascaleon was impressed and touched by the sincerity and ardour of his young charge. He bent slowly on one knee.

"There was no way for you to know my pledge, unless a messenger of the gods told you. But I was really testing you to see how firmly you were set on doing this. As it is, I want to be next to you, no, in front of you in any battle. There are many good knights and veteran fighters around your father. I know their techniques. Old I am, but I know better than you, which blow must be avoided and which to expect; when to strike and when to block. I have practised swords fighting all my life. Let's get you ready for the fight of your life."

Chapter Thirteen

Ascaleon brought Florio into his armoury and showed him all the fighting equipment he needed. First, he began to arm him with beautiful, yet solid armour. After clothing him in a thick jupon of red silk, he made him wear two new mail stockings and two sharp spurs. On the stockings he put a pair of greaves to cover the shins and calves, and a pair of cuisses for the thighs. After slipping on the sleeves and fastening the tassets over the hips, he placed a gorget to protect his neck. Then he covered his torso with a pair of very light plates, lined with red velvet as befitting a nobleman. He sheathed his arms with fine vambraces and cubitieres. The magic swords came next, fastened around his waist. On his head he placed a basinet-shaped skull cap with a handsome strong camail upon which he fitted a light helmet studded with precious stones and engraved with a gold eagle's outspread wings. He also gave him a pair of gauntlet gloves as required for such armour. Finally, he covered his left shoulder with a fine shield, shining with gold, in which were fielded six red stones. That completed Florio's armament. Now he needed some basic training. And Ascaleon was ready to give it to his young pupil. Armed with lance and sword, which he used to demonstrate his instructions, he spoke to him firmly.

"My dear son, just as you listened to my teachings in science and courtly behaviour, follow me closely now, for what I am about to teach you will save your life.

"When you come into a field against an enemy, take to the high ground as much as you can, so you will look down at him, not vice versa.

"Do not face the sun's rays for they can blind you, but have your shield face the sun to blind your enemy. Likewise, do not go into a dusty wind that may greatly hinder your visibility.

"Do not ride your horse at a fast pace when far away from the enemy. Go slowly at first and pick up speed when you are closing in on them. Let the horse run the distance with his head stretched out, but don't give him yet the bit all the way because he would go with less power if his neck is stretched out.

"Do not lower the lance at the start of the fight because a cunning enemy would take cover from your expected strike. Plus, your arm will be tired from the lance's weight before you get to him.

"Take cover from his first strike, approach him quickly, lower the lance, and try to aim toward the throat rather than the top of his helmet. Low blows hurt more than the high ones, even if they are not spectacular.

"If you want to hurt him with your horse, make sure you don't run into the chest of his horse as the damage could be reciprocal. Instead, circle around to direct the chest of your horse against the left shoulder of his and strike there; it won't hurt yours.

"When the lances are no longer used or useful, pull out your sword quickly.

"Don't strike too many blows—just a few powerful ones—until you see your adversary tiring or falling under you. Only then the blows must *not* be spared.

"Always shield yourself, even when attacking. The enemy looks for open targets.

"Do not let yourself be grappled, but, if it happens, do not try to fell him on the ground immediately. Instead, holding strongly on to him, let him exert himself until he is quite breathless. Then you can more easily draw all your strength and defeat him.

"Do not let his screaming or any other noise distract you, but keep your eyes open to all things about you.

"Show confidence and never fear anyone else. Fear does not kill, but it can paralyse you. Besides, with your armour and sword, and me next to you, you have nothing to fear."

To all that, Florio had only one comment. "Master, I hear you and obey you. But it is very late. We must move fast. So please, arm yourself and let us go on our mission. Biancofiore awaits."

Ascaleon lost no time in doing so. But while he was

selecting arms and saddling horses, Florio began practising with his sword and lance. There was something uncanny about the way he used those weapons, as if he had been trained with them for a long time. Ascaleon noticed with a smile that his pupil was more than a mere boy in shiny armour. He was a young knight in need of a fight.

When the horses were ready, Ascaleon brought out two hooded coats that covered their armour, put them on each other, and then they left the stables. Their fast horses brought them to town before daybreak. Although Florio was eager to run in and attack the whole garrison, Ascaleon suggested they wait outside the gates not to attract undue attention from the guards. They pretended to sleep, but they could not.

Only a short distance away, Biancofiore had fallen asleep after a night of tears and anguish at not being able to talk to anyone and find out why she was being accused of such a hideous treachery. She received the answer in a dream.

Suddenly, the darkness of her dungeon was illuminated by pink, purple, and golden lights, but more than lights they were heavenly clouds from which emerged the goddess Venus, naked but for a purple veil floating about her body. With laurels as a crown and an olive branch in her hand, she spoke soothingly to Biancofiore.

"My beautiful young lady, do not despair. Nothing

will happen to you, except for a bit of fear running through your human body. I will never abandon you. Never."

Encouraged by Venus' presence and promise, Biancofiore had only one question.

"What is the reason for all this happening to me?"

Venus smiled knowingly. "No other reason but because you and Florio have placed yourselves at my service. The plot against you is contrived and evil, but I have planned your deliverance; soon you will be restored to the king's favour and to your accustomed grace. I will tell you no more now. You will see and know all tomorrow."

She disappeared, but a semblance of light and colours was left to illuminate the cell until Biancofiore was taken out of it to be led to death.

Chapter Fourteen

It seems that nobody slept much or well that night, including the king, who, as soon as the sun arose, summoned the judges and ordered them to condemn Biancofiore without delay. But the judges had taken pity on Biancofiore and tried to help her out of her predicament.

"Most High Lord, no person can be judged by us if she does not confess her guilt openly. As we have not heard a word from Biancofiore, her death sentence might fall back on our heads if we do not follow the judicial order of due process."

The king was very upset by these unexpected words. He did not want Biancofiore to be heard and did not want Florio to hear of this. So he rebuffed them.

"The crime she committed needs no confession since it was so manifest that even if she wanted, she could not deny it. Therefore, you must judge her at once."

The judges were terror-stricken and cowered at the king's authority. They turned to the guards and ordered them, "Bring Biancofiore here."

Biancofiore was brought in. She was dressed in

black, as befitted a noble lady, but the judges now treated her like a common criminal, as they voiced their sentence.

"Let it be known to all that the present wicked maiden Biancofiore by deceit and treachery wanted this past day to poison our and her lord, King Felix, with a peacock, under the pretext of honouring him. And in order that no one may ever attempt such a crime, we condemn her to be burned until she becomes common ashes, which then will be thrown to the wind. Guards, take her to the stake without delay."

As Biancofiore, crying and grieving silently, was being led away, she saw the queen and the king watching the proceedings from a nearby portal. To them she raised her voice, not suppliantly, but forgivingly.

"Dear father, King Felix, who gave me and my mother grace and honour in the past, although we were foreigners, may you and the queen remain in the grace of the gods whom I pray to forgive you for my unjust death. May they be more propitious to you than they have been toward me."

Her charitable words infuriated the seneschal riding on a tall horse and wielding a stick in his hand. He came up and beat the guards who were hesitating in carrying out the judges' order swiftly enough.

"Go on. Take her to the stake. Her words mean nothing to you or anybody else."

The guards then began pulling Biancofiore roughly

and unceremoniously toward the Braa Square where the fire had already been prepared. But the people, clearly touched by Biancofiore's words and her unjust sentence, began voicing their displeasure loudly and angrily. The seneschal then ordered the guards to form a large circle around the fire so that the executioners could do their duty without impediment. The opening of the circle revealed the presence of two knights approaching Biancofiore as if to defend her. Biancofiore, without knowing any more about them than anyone else, imagined one of them to be Florio coming there for her deliverance. But what was that reddish light in front of them? Could it be Venus? For the first time since the banquet she began to feel comfort and hope in her salvation.

Chapter Fifteen

As they were slowly riding toward the centre of the square where the fire was already burning, Ascaleon noticed a strange red cloud preceding them, almost pacing them. Curious, but not afraid, he asked Florio about it. "Are my old eyes playing tricks on me, or do I see something red ahead of us?"

"Something red?" repeated Florio, almost deriding him." That *something* is taller than all men, very fierce, with a very long beard, and so bright red that I can barely look at him. Don't you recognise Mars when you see him?"

"Your description fits him perfectly from what I have read about him. But I only see a strange light, not a god," replied Ascaleon with some reservation. "And where did you get that bow and arrows? They were not in our armoury room, ever. I would have stormed a fortress to get such splendid weapons."

"Mars gave them to me this morning, while you were sleeping. And he told me: no enemy will be so distant that you may not reach him with this dart if you merely see him. Foolish is he who awaits it, daring he who shoots it, and a god he who made it."

"Now I believe without any doubt what you told me last night," replied Ascaleon solemnly. "Although until now I have had some strong doubts about the truth of your words. The gods love you. Great deeds await you."

Thus, talking and following the divine knight, they reached the square where the flames were already burning. Having crossed into the great circle that the seneschal had made around the fire, they stopped to see if anyone opposed them. No one did. The strange redness struck fear and wonder in everyone's hearts.

Even the seneschal was afraid, although he could not show such weakness. So he approached the strangers and with an angry voice he ordered, "Gentlemen, move back."

Mars warned Florio, "Young knight, this is the enemy you must defeat today. He is the one who carried out your parents' evil scheme. Answer him, but do not move back."

Florio was eager to comply. He came forward with as much fierceness as if he had wanted to kill him immediately and said, "Treacherous knight, neither you nor the others will make me move from here one step more than I want to."

The seneschal realised the gravity of his situation and pulled back to look for greater help.

As Florio watched him leave the circle, he noticed that a guard had seized Biancofiore and was about to throw her into the fire. Seeing her dressed in black, her beautiful eyes full of tears, her blonde hair twisted and wrapped carelessly around her head, her delicate hands tied with strong ropes, her gentle body mishandled by vile people almost made him cry, but he turned his emotion into anger as he struck his horse with his spurs, breaking through the packed crowd, which had quickly moved into the circle vacated by the seneschal and yelled at the guards.

"Untie her hands and don't touch her again if your life is dear to you."

The guards obeyed immediately and moved away from her.

Florio, his face still covered by his helmet, then spoke to her in a loud voice. "Young maiden, abandon every fear for the gods that love you brought me here to defend you. Whatever the reason you are here, I promise you that as long as I and my companion breathe, we will protect you for the love of Florio—whom I love as much as myself—and your graciousness."

He then rose his helmet's visor just enough to speak more clearly to the crowd, without being recognised.

"My good people, Florio asked me to help defend Biancofiore against the false accusation for which she was almost killed. She did nothing more than carry out the orders of the seneschal. He is the one who plotted the crime and should be sentenced, not she. Whoever may disagree with this, I am eager to prove wrong in combat and risk my life to uphold her innocence."

Many noble men in the crowd who had also been at the banquet agreed that she should not be punished for following orders, and they sent messengers to inform the king. One of the judges in the crowd ordered that the sentence should not proceed any further until the young knight had proved his intentions.

But the seneschal objected to those motions in a forceful way.

"The knight lies through his teeth. Biancofiore is guilty and must be punished, no matter what Florio or any god might do to help her." And he ordered the guards to put her immediately into the fire.

Florio spoke directly to the guards. "As I warned you, touch her and you die. Let this dog bark as much as he wants. If he wishes her to die, let him come forward and touch her."

In response, the seneschal, full of anger and hatred, spurred his horse toward Florio. "Who are you to oppose our power with such outrageous words? If you speak further, I will have you seized and burned together with her. Away. Be gone from here immediately, knave!"

Unable to hold his anger any more, Florio hit him on the head with his gauntleted fist hard enough to make him fall on the saddle's pommel quite stunned. Florio then raised himself on the stirrups and wrapped his arm around him to throw him into the burning fire, but the seneschal's many helpers aided him to escape from

Florio's grasp.

Once free, the seneschal galloped furiously into the royal palace and without apology disrupted the noblemen's accounts of the events in the square, and spoke to the king.

"Your Majesty, pay no attention to what they say and listen to me. Your edict is being challenged by a rude, armoured knight, and his friend, who wants to prove to me by force of arms Biancofiore's innocence and his loyalty to Florio. As a result, he will not leave without doing battle to rescue her or to die in the process. Therefore, I beg you, grant me the right of battle with new arms and a horse to preserve your honour in front of the whole city and to restore mine, vilified when he attacked me while I was disarmed."

His furrowed forehead clearly revealed the king's anger and disappointment. Who could that knight be? Why did the gods allow his plans to go awry? He needed time to think and to know. He forced himself to speak calmly to the seneschal.

"Massamutino, it seems to me that the hour is very late for doing battle, and you appear to be very tired. So let us suspend the battle until tomorrow. Invite the knight to eat and be our honoured guest until morning, when you will fight him since we cannot deny him battle."

"Sire," answered the seneschal. "In no way can the battle be avoided today. The knight is so fierce that he will fight anyone wanting to touch Biancofiore. Even if you order a delay, if I'd try to bring her back to prison, I would have to fight him. I pray you, therefore, to let me do it now since I am so full of animosity against him."

The king shook his head as he did not like what he heard, but had no other option. "Since the battle cannot be stopped today, go and take any arms and horses that you like, and see that you earn honour with a victory. Remember that the truth of our words is in your hands."

He then beckoned him to come closer so that the other people could not hear him and whispered into his ear, "Order the guards to throw Biancofiore in the burning fire while the crowd is watching your fight. Once that is done, do not worry at all about your victory."

"This will be done within my power," answered the seneschal, his eyes glowing with diabolical joy as he bowed to the king and left the room to arm himself for combat.

Chapter Sixteen

While Biancofiore was looking at her rescuer, trying to figure out who he was among the many friends he had, the seneschal arrived on the square, fully armed with two companions, each riding a tall horse. One of them was carrying for him a strong shield on which was etched a rampant lion of gold in a blue field, and the other carried a short and heavy lance with pennants bearing the same coat of arms.

To both of them he whispered, "Remember what I told you to do while I am in combat."

His companions nodded and moved closer to Biancofiore.

The crowd, although excited by the imminent confrontation, had questions and reservations.

"Who is this knight? Doesn't he sound young? Is he strong enough to put an end to the seneschal's arrogance?"

Florio heard that last remark and reassured the speaker by raising his lance in salute. He then spoke soothingly to Biancofiore. "Oh, fair maiden, here is my adversary. There can be no more delay to do battle, but be confident because the time of your deliverance has come." To his companions—the god and the teacher—he entrusted Biancofiore. "Look after her and make sure that, while I fight, no harm comes to her."

Having said that, he picked up his lance, moved his horse as far back as he thought necessary, turned around, and waited for the seneschal to do the same at the other end.

Mars appeared suddenly at Florio's side. "Young knight, this is the time to show the valour of your daring heart. Follow the teachings of your tutor and attack. Your enemy is armed and already on the move."

And with that Mars breathed on his face, fixed the strong lance in his hand, and returned to his red cloud.

Florio took one last look at Biancofiore before he struck his horse with the spurs, directing it toward the enemy coming fast with his lance lowered.

The people watching could barely see the galloping of Florio's horse, so fast he alighted on the seneschal. He struck him on the throat and threw him to the ground so harshly that his lance broke.

He had just inflicted the blow when the guards, seeing the people completely intent on the fight, approached Biancofiore to do as ordered. But Mars, aware of their intentions, ran luminously to her and enveloped her in his light, causing the guards to run away with fright.

The seneschal, meanwhile, had recovered from the blow only to find himself on the ground with his lance still in hand, but no enemy around. He then heard an approaching gallop and saw the bright knight coming at him, indeed talking to him. "Your arrogance is greater than your skills to fare so poorly in our first round."

To which the seneschal replied, "I would not fare any worse than you if I had a horse; but you will not have that advantage much longer."

And he quickly raised his sword to wound Florio on the head. But his rash blow fell short and landed on the neck of Florio's horse, nearly decapitating it.

As the horse fell dead, Florio jumped off it, pulled out his heavenly sword, and bumped the seneschal with his chest forcibly enough to make any man fall. But the stout seneschal regained his balance, in turn pushing Florio with his chest, not letting him come near him, while striking him constantly with heavy blows.

Florio kept blocking those blows with his shining shield, so they hurt him little or not at all. Remembering Ascaleon's teachings, he kept looking for a way to inflict one mortal blow at the throat, where his lance had broken through the armour's mail. When the chance came, Florio struck vigorously, thrusting the sword deeply into the naked flesh and throwing the seneschal to the ground.

All spectators shouted, "The seneschal is dead; Biancofiore is free. The seneschal is dead."

But he was not. Stunned, but not killed, the seneschal rose to his feet, climbed on a horse taken from his aides, and began to flee.

When Florio, heading toward Biancofiore, saw that, he became angered at himself for not having completed his task. Quickly he picked up his bow, put in an arrow, pulled it back and shot it after him, shouting, "Even if your horse could fly, this will reach you faster than you think."

It did. The arrow struck the rider in the kidney and threw him off the horse. Florio ran to him, took him by his rough beard, and dragged him unceremoniously to the burning fire, leaving a trail of blood on the ground.

He stopped a few steps from the fire and told him, "If you want us to have any pity on you, tell these people how the poisoned peacock was sent to the king and why this innocent maiden was blamed."

The seneschal was held up by his guards so the people could see him and hear when he spoke.

"I loved Biancofiore above all things in the world, and asked the king to give her to me in marriage. She refused to have a vile man like me and begged the king not to relent. The king agreed with her. That's when my love turned into hatred and revenge. I wanted her to die young and miserably. So I poisoned the peacock and ordered her to take it to the king. I did this to kill her, but this knight has rescued her by winning our fight."

The seneschal did not mention the king's complicity in the plot, believing that he would remain in the king's good grace if he survived. Florio, on the other hand, was glad that his father's role was not publicly revealed. But as soon as the seneschal was silent, everyone shouted, "Let him die; let him die."

Upon hearing the people's shouting, Florio looked to his companions for advice.

Mars, still visible only to Florio, read him the verdict. "For such a man, one must have no mercy, lest justice suffer because of our intervention. Let this be the last moment of his life. Throw him into the fire that he had prepared for the innocent Biancofiore."

Upon hearing Mars' command, Florio took the seneschal by the beard and threw him into the crackling fire.

Thus, the sinister life of the king's seneschal ended amid loud screams and grievous pains.

Chapter Seventeen

After throwing the seneschal into the flames, Florio
helped Biancofiore mount on a beautiful steed and, with
his companions, rode toward the royal palace. When
Biancofiore realised where they were headed, she began
trembling with apprehension.

"Where do you take me now, valorous knight, back
to the most dangerous place for me? Then why did you
save me? And if you are such a good friend of Florio,
why not take me back to Montorio? I will be much
happier if you return me to him than to his father."

Florio, struggling to keep his voice deep and
diverse, tried to reassure her.

"Gracious maiden, do not fear. The gods want you
to be returned to King Felix so that he will regret his
mistake and amend for it by restoring you to your past
honours. Besides, Florio will come to see you or send
for you immediately."

Biancofiore sighed deeply, and shrugged her
shoulders, hoping that he was right.

When they arrived at the royal palace, the king,
surrounded by the nobles who were briefing him on the
morning's events, rose and went to meet them, feigning

great happiness.

Florio bowed to the king and spoke without raising his visor.

"Sire, I commend unto you this maiden whom I, with the help of the gods, have just freed from an unjust sentence. I pray you shall find no more occasions to act against her as you did yesterday. Since truth is always known at the end, you may accrue deserved infamy. Also be mindful that when you demand her death, you demand Florio's death as well. Therefore, hold her more dearly than you have until now."

Having said that, he placed her in his hands and withdrew.

The king embraced her and kissed her on the forehead as one who had just found a dear missing daughter.

Biancofiore, shaking uncontrollably, threw herself at his feet, kissed them, and kneeling before him cried, "Dear father and lord, if I ever offended you in anything, forgive me because I did so out of ignorance, not malice. I had no blame in what happened yesterday. The culprit confessed before his death. Therefore, dear father and lord, reinvest me with your grace of which I was unjustly deprived."

For the second time the king embraced her as he held her up on her feet.

"Say no more. You were never as dear and welcome to me as you are now." Then he turned to

Florio. "For your courage in making us see the truth and for your friendship with my son, I would like to know who you are, if that does not annoy you. But I can promise you that the young maiden will always be taken good care of."

"At the present it is not possible for me to tell you who I am; therefore, forgive me. And with your permission, I will gladly depart with my companions."

The king agreed with a sigh of relief. Meddling strangers were not favourite guests.

"Since I cannot know who you are, go in peace, and may the gods watch over you forever more."

Florio looked at Biancofiore once more, but her face was blurred by his tears. He and his party took leave of the king, descended the stairs, mounted on their horses and left the town. Just outside the gates, Mars turned to him, stopped, and announced, "Now that you have accomplished what we came here for, I must return to my place as you two must return to Montorio."

Florio and Ascaleon immediately dismounted from their horses, threw themselves at the god's feet and thanked him for his immeasurable help. And while they were offering thanks and praises, Mars suddenly disappeared from their sight. The young man and his teacher climbed back on their horses and returned to Montorio while the sun was still bright in the sky.

During the following week, Florio—eager to show his gratitude for the successful rescue of Biancofiore—

honoured all the temples in town with gifts, flowers, and sacrifices for every god in the Pantheon. Everyone, except Diana. She was not pleased to be overlooked, even accidentally, by the eager youth. And a slighted goddess never forgets. Or forgives.

Chapter Eighteen

Life away from Biancofiore was at best miserable for Florio. At worst, it was a way of subsisting from day to week, from week to month, *ad infinitum* it seemed, especially after being so near to her for such a brief time after a long separation. Indeed, the brief encounter revived an even greater passion for her, for her presence, for her chaste kisses and words. Florio tried to distract himself by visiting friends and attending their gatherings, but the results were always the same. Making busy time with friends made him more anxious to be alone and think about Biancofiore. What was she doing? Whom was she visiting? What young men were courting her? Beautiful as she was to admire and pleasant as she could be to speak to, she must have had many suitors escorting her through the royal gardens. The king, to be sure, would greatly encourage such encounters in the hope that she might find some man attractive enough to make her forget Florio. The mind of Florio was so tormented by these and other thoughts that he could hardly hide his grief or enjoy any pleasure. His vitality had grown so weak that food or sleep had become unimportant to him. His face pale and emaciated, his limbs thinned, he lay down most of the day, like people afflicted by a long illness seeking new things and liking none, and if they like something, they cannot eat it or enjoy it.

The duke and Ascaleon were desperate for a solution to Florio's problem, but knew not what to do. If they told the king, he might blame Biancofiore for his malaise and harm her again. If they said nothing, someone else might inform the king, who would then be justly angered by their failure to report directly to him.

One day, as they discussed various approaches, the duke asked Ascaleon, "What would you do in a battle if your troops were too preoccupied with personal problems to take up arms and fight like warriors?"

"Why, I would distract them with something that would take their minds off whatever bothered them. Maybe a wrestling match. Maybe Egyptian dancers."

The duke pondered for a while and then a smile came upon his face.

"That's what we need for Florio. A distraction. Entertainment. Dancers? No, too young for that. But close enough." He walked around the room several times and stopped, with a greater smile on his face. "And what is a substitute for a lover pining over his distant beloved?" Without waiting for an answer, he added, "Another lover. But one with something stronger added to the recipe. A beautiful woman willing to make him forget that which he doesn't have for something which he can have: the pleasures of the flesh."

Ascaleon was horrified. "Florio would never agree to betray Biancofiore for another woman."

"I said nothing about betrayal," huffed the duke. "Just taking his mind off of her for a while and acting normal again would do. To make the temptation stronger, I would bring in two women instead of one. Give him a choice or overwhelm him with more attractions."

Ascaleon thought about it for a moment before he nodded his agreement.

"It might just work. Look. If he happens to forget Biancofiore through someone else, it would be easier to take that someone else out of his heart than to remove Biancofiore now. New wounds can be cured better and faster than old ones."

Having agreed on their plan, they set out to find some maiden who would look as much as possible like Biancofiore. They reasoned that such a person would be more to his liking than others and nudge him closer to their desired goals. Through a friend of a friend they found not one, but two such beauties that had been eyeing Florio since his arrival in Montorio, but had not approached him because, though aristocratic, they were not at a princely level. Ascaleon suggested summoning both of them.

"Since they both like Florio, each will try harder to make Florio like her. Besides, where one might fail, the other will succeed."

The duke liked the idea and brought the ladies in under the pretext of inviting them to a feast. When they arrived, the duke spoke to them in a comforting and casual tone.

"Young ladies, we are about to give Florio the company of a beautiful wife. After searching the city, we found that there was none better than you in beauty, manners, and reputation. We think that you can distract him from some preoccupation he has at the moment and make him happy. The one he likes the best we will give him as his wife."

Edea, the more vivacious of the two, was quick to answer. "Lord, we know that we are not of royal blood befitting Florio's rank, nor have we the large dowries that easily cover the shortcomings of many noble ladies. So please do not make fun of us. Your proposal can bring us only shame and dishonour."

The duke got up in seeming agitation and outrage, went directly in front of the ladies and even bowed to them before he spoke with courtly indignation.

"Ladies, do not think for one moment that I would consider urging you to such depravity as to lose your honour. I swear on my father's soul and our gods that he will marry either one of you he likes the most."

He turned around to look at Ascaleon, who nodded in total agreement, and sat down again. The two ladies whispered in each other's ears several times before Edea again spoke for both of them.

"Lord duke, since you promise it on an oath, we will do your pleasure. Just tell us how and when it will be done."

"This is the way," answered the duke. "Dressed in your best style, just the two of you will come to that garden below where he goes in the afternoon when the sun is too hot. Meet him there by the main fountain and talk to him and entertain him in any way you believe might please him most. Then whoever accomplishes that will win. Doesn't that seem fair to you?"

Convinced by the eloquence and mannerism of the duke, the ladies accepted the challenge, each hoping to best the other in their quest of a lifetime. It would take place on the next day in the Ducal Garden.

Chapter Nineteen

The garden was as beautiful as Eden must have been: evergreen trees, fruits and flowers, fresh grass bathed by gurgling fountains and streams, birds sweetly singing and butterflies flying everywhere. The two young women marvelled at the beauty of the place and made garlands with grape leaves, while walking around. Dressed with very thin clothes, their hair arranged by expert hands, they resembled Greek goddesses when they sat near a stately fountain and raised their voices in a lovely song. Pretty as they were, they could sing just as prettily.

Florio heard them, as he approached his favourite reading spot, and quickened his steps to see who could possibly be there. "Biancofiore? Venus?" he murmured. Then he saw them: two beautiful ladies, with very white bodies and rosy faces, eyes like morning stars and small mouths, the colour of vermillion roses, made more seductive by modulating the notes of their song. Their hair was very blonde, with threads of gold, somewhat curly, cascading upon their slender necks. Their thin dresses—with a sash at the waist enhancing the globules of their beautiful breasts pushing out of their tight camisole—had various slits through which their porcelain flesh could be seen. Florio stopped, completely confused by the wondrous sight. They too stopped singing when they saw him and rose to curtsey to him.

"May the gods give you a full day of happiness," he greeted them.

"They already have with your arrival," they replied in unison.

"Then why did you stop your enjoyment when I arrived?"

"No greater enjoyment could we have than to be with you."

"What were you two doing here all by yourselves?"

"Our group went ahead when we became tired. They'll be back before sunset. But we were really hoping to see you. We are lucky we did."

"Lucky is the one whom the gods will allow to possess such beauties."

"Lucky and blessed, indeed," they replied and came closer to him.

One put her head in his lap and the other stretched her arm upon his neck. They fawned over him and caressed him gently, almost timidly. He seemed to enjoy their amorous attention. Often with subtle glances he would direct his eyes between the white robes and the pink flesh and see more openly that which the thin clothes did not cover. Sometimes he touched their white throats with a trembling hand; at other times he strived to slip his fingers between the cleavages of their dresses and find their breasts. He probed each new part of their bodies with joyful tact. Nothing was denied him. And soon they became intimate enough with him (and he with them) that nothing but shame restrained them from reaching the ultimate that can be asked of a lover. Then something happened.

Was it a premonition? A god's intervention? Or simply the smile on the girls' faces that reminded him of Biancofiore? Biancofiore! The living dream crashed into rancour.

In the heat of the moment, the younger girl, Calmena, suddenly raised her head and looked at Florio with a troubled expression. "Say, Florio. Why is your face so pale right now? Is something troubling you?"

Florio could not answer her. In his mind he was questioning his behaviour. *Would I like it if someone else behaved like that toward Biancofiore? Did she deserve to be treated like that? How could I love her so much and even think of touching another woman? If she knew this, wouldn't she have reasons not to want to see me any more?*

Calmena asked him again, "Answer me, my soul. Why are you so sad? Why do you move away from me who loves you more than herself?"

"Please, ladies, let me be. Other matters trouble my mind at the moment."

"And what is worrying you so suddenly? One moment you are cordial, talkative, and approachable. The next you are sullen and can't even look at us. Why, pray tell us?"

Florio answered nothing, but kept turning his face away from them, as if afraid of the beauties he was just admiring and touching. But as he moved away from them, they moved even closer to him and behaved more amorously.

Of the two, Calmena who was already inflamed beyond propriety, embraced him tightly and could not restrain herself from kissing him.

"My gracious lord, why do you not tell us the reason for this sudden melancholy? Aren't we pleasing you or beautiful enough for you? Why do you refuse us?"

They tried to resume the touching and caressing that had excited him a while before. Florio would have none of it. He pushed them away and asked them sternly, "Tell me, ladies, were you ever in love?"

"Yes, but with you only. We never felt this passionate with anyone else."

"You are not in love with me or anyone else or you wouldn't behave in this way. Love is shy until familiarity makes the hearts recognise each other as equal. True love would not allow for such intimacy at a first meeting. So let me be. Do with me anything you would do with a friend or a servant, anything but love."

When she heard this, Edea erupted into tears and ripped her thin dress. "How can you not believe that my heart aches for your love? If I seemed too eager to fulfil my desires, it was only because my excessive love for you overcame my modesty and made me delirious. I am ashamed, forlorn, and hurt. Just kill me now so I will not live in misery forever."

Florio could not turn away from such a sad lady.

"Sweet, sweet lady, do not ruin your face with bitter tears. I am sure a more gracious man will grant your wishes. I swear by the gods that if I did not belong to someone, no one else but you would have me. But I can't give what is not mine to give."

Undeterred by Florio's gentleness, Calmena spoke angrily, "How can you deny us what we ask of you? Are you meaner than a beast? No love promise can be so strong that it could not be broken by our pleas. Do you think that if we suffer because of your indifference, your woman—if you have one—will love you more for it? She would definitely hate you for being so cruel to another woman."

To which Edea added, "How can you deny us at least kisses, which you gave us gladly a moment ago? Grant us some love and the gods will be more willing to grant your wishes, if anything else is desired by you right now."

Florio had had enough. "Stop this nonsense at once. I belong completely to only one, so do not ask me for anything since you could get from me nothing but pain. Just leave me alone. Now."

Florio's resolute manner convinced the two ladies to give up on him. They dressed quickly and practically ran inside to meet the duke. They told him what had happened with no little shame. In return they received no little gifts. They left the ducal palace richer and sadder, but perhaps a little wiser about the vagaries of young princes in love with someone who was not even around. If she even existed.

Chapter Twenty

As soon as the girls had left, the duke summoned Ascaleon and together walked quickly toward Florio's favourite place. They found him in deep thoughts—so much so that he did not even acknowledge their presence until Ascaleon extended his hand, took him by his arm, and shook him gently.

"Loving boy, where are you now? Are you so troubled or so out of yourself that you do not even bother to greet us?"

Florio raised his head as if awakening from a deep sleep. "What brings you here to disrupt my thoughts? Comforting words can only add to my misery. Please leave me alone."

"Love and worry lead us here," replied Ascaleon. "And we will not leave you until you give us the new reason for your unhappiness."

Florio shook his head. "There is no new reason for my grief. Love alone keeps me in this mood."

It was the duke's turn to be perplexed. "I thought you were following my advice when you received those girls so nicely. Instead you are back to your usual way. It does not make sense to blame it on love. I actually am concerned about your sanity. People in love try to numb their pain with various pleasures. You appear to increase yours with more pains. Share your troubles with us so that their burden will not be so heavy for you alone."

Florio embraced them both before he spoke.

"Friends, I know you are concerned about my health and my sanity. Maybe you can understand my plight if I tell you about it. First of all, I want to see Biancofiore more than anything else. The more I think about her, the angrier I get for being sent away from her. Then I live in constant fear that my parents might harm her again. Most of all, being so beautiful, she attracts men like a siren. Sooner or later she might take another man since she cannot see me or be with me. And you wonder why I can't partake of the pleasures around me? Believe me: my only food and joy are to think of her. It gives my body whatever life is still in me. If you prize that life, do not take away from me the privilege to think about her."

The duke smiled at him like an understanding father to a troubled son.

"We are bothered by the kinds of thoughts you harbour. First of all, stop nurturing morbid thoughts and start thinking about the joys of life. It's one way to get rid of Melancholy, the black bile humour that poisons young lovers. But let's look at the maelstrom you are putting yourself in.

"You grieve because you cannot see Biancofiore. I believe you. But does that help you see her any sooner? Not one bit. Remember: Fortune does not hold her wheel still forever. She took you away from her; she will bring her back in her next spin.

"As for her health, love never caused death when the two sides were of one will. Should she get sick like you out of love? Would you want that? Of course not, so forget it.

"As for the king, he swears that he loves Biancofiore as much as a daughter, but he would quickly blame her if anything happened to you.

"You mentioned jealousy? She loves you, and what woman, loved by a young man like you—handsome, rich, and a future king—would be so foolish as to leave you for any other?

"You say that women always take to bad boys. Not all, and that applies also to men taking to bad girls. Biancofiore is smarter than that.

"So, taking all this into consideration, who should be happier than you? You have everything going for you: looks, status, youth, wealth, and a beauty who loves you. If I were you, I would take very good care of myself so that I would live and love her for a long time. Why worry about things that have not happened? Be happy. Smart people always find the way and the wisdom to feel good about themselves."

Never was Florio happier to hear such words of

wisdom and comfort coming from a caring relative. Finally, with a smile on his face, he embraced them effusively.

"Friends, you are right. We can hardly fight against sudden tragedies, let alone cry before they come. Whatever my father plans to do, I will take your advice and stop worrying about future events."

With that, they walked out of the garden—for the stars had already punctured the dark sky with their lights—and returned almost happy to their rooms. For the first time in months, Florio slept soundly and comfortably all night. If he only knew what nightmare would follow!

Chapter Twenty-One

Not long after Biancofiore's ordeal by fire, a young knight named Fileno came to visit the court of King Felix. He was noble, handsome, virtuous and well-mannered—in sum, a great prospect for the ladies of the court. In him the king and queen saw an opportunity for distracting Biancofiore from her longing for Florio, something that they were very well aware of by now. As soon as Fileno met the bright beauty of Biancofiore, he was smitten by and fell helplessly in love with her. From that day on he tried to please her in various ways, with words, songs, compliments and gracious ceremonies. However, Biancofiore was not interested in him and pretended that she was not aware of his feelings. But the queen had other ideas. Hoping that Biancofiore might eventually be attracted to him, she often summoned him to their presence while Biancofiore was there—which was every day.

In response Biancofiore sighed bashfully and lowered her head as she came before Fileno while the king was holding court. Fileno assumed that she was sighing for him. Biancofiore did not actually dissuade him. In fact, she began to pretend to like the young knight if only to soothe the irascible queen, when a new event came into play.

As the feast in honour of Mars was approaching, it was customary to celebrate it with jousting games that showcased the strength and valour of young knights. Fileno, eager to impress Biancofiore, entered the contest and asked her for a token to wear as his combat colours. He made his demand in front of the court.

"Gracious maiden, whose beauty moulded by Jupiter I cannot resist, I pray that for the coming jousting you give me any of your valuables, which I'll wear as my colours and will give me more strength and daring than I already have to attain victory for the love of you."

Not knowing what to do, she turned to the queen with questioning eyes. The queen promptly chided her. "Young lady, raise your head. Why are you ashamed? There is no other woman in town as beautiful as you. Since he asks you a favour as someone who wishes to serve you out of love, you cannot deny him. Kindly give him one of your things, like the veil you are wearing on your head now. If things go wrong, you can always say that he got it from another woman, since there are many similar ones."

Compelled by the looks, more than the words, of the queen, Biancofiore unravelled the veil from her blonde head and, sighing, gave it to Fileno. He received it with so much grace that one would believe he had never received a greater gift. He tied it around his head and went into combat. Because of his skills or the veil's inspiration, no one defeated him. As a result, he was crowned the tournament's winner when golden laurels were placed upon the veil. The queen was overjoyed. Fileno was in ecstasy. Biancofiore was embarrassed. Again, her red-faced bashfulness was taken by Fileno as a sign of secret admiration... which was not entirely untrue as Biancofiore began to see her beloved Florio in his face. She missed his company, his witty remarks, his adoring stares, his irreplaceable tenderness. If she closed her eyes, she could hear loving words from the sweet lips she ached to kiss. But then too, there was something strange about Fileno, a vague sense of danger that she could not explain or cast out. She tried to stay away from him, but the damage was done.

As the fates would have it, a few days later Fileno travelled to Montorio where he was received with great honours in the hall of the duke. There he told everyone around how he had earned a jousting victory and the love of the town's most beautiful girl during the Mars Festival in Marmorina. The crowd of young knights was eager to hear the details of the contest and of the beautiful damsel whose colours were worn by Fileno. The crowd's noise attracted the attention of Florio, who, of late, was always with the duke.

When Florio heard the name of Marmorina, he felt as if a lance had pierced his heart. Still, he maintained his composure and eventually was able to pull Fileno out of the crowd and take him to his room, under the pretext of wanting to know more about his travels around the world.

But after a short while, Florio decided to get to the point in question. And he began a delicate approach to learn what he wanted, while fearing the truth.

"From your looks and actions, you seem to be a person in love. Or am I reading too much on your face?"

"My lord, I love more than all the other young men in town."

"That pleases me very much, as I feel the same. But say, does the lady love you?"

"Nothing pleases me more than being loved by her."

"But how do you know that she loves you? Did she tell you that?"

"I know she loves me for three reasons. First, by her timid glancing and sighing in my presence. Next by a precious gift, which would never be given without love by a lady, and thirdly, by the joy I see on her pretty face when something good happens to me."

"But what did she give you that was so important and meaningful?"

"When I asked for a token to take into the contest, she gave this." Fileno pulled Biancofiore's veil from his pocket. "Then she wished that I'd do well for the love of her. Isn't that a clear sign of true love?"

"Indeed, it is. But is this lady beautiful? Does she have a name? Do I know her?"

"When I tell you her name, you'll have the answer to all your questions. She lives in your father's royal palace as the queen's lady-in-waiting. You know her, so I do not need to tell you how beautiful she is. Her name is Biancofiore."

Without changing the expression on his face Florio warned him. "Because you are so sincere, I will give you some advice. Love wisely, but not so completely that you can't stop loving her if she changes her mind. Like you I loved and still love a beautiful lady. She gave me this ring in place of true love. Then she left me and pledged herself to another man, but I cannot forget her or stop loving her. Don't let that happen to you."

Fileno looked at Florio straight in the eyes and said, "Your advice is good, but I know this lady is so honest that she will not change her intention to love me."

"Then you are luckier than most men and happier than any god."

Florio turned away and went into another room as tears welled in his eyes.

That night, sleep came very late and very slowly, but when it did, it brought Florio a wondrous dream. Or was it a vision?

The vision opened on a beautiful plain in the middle of which sat a great lord, with a golden crown and wearing royal vestments. He held a strong bow in his left hand and two arrows in his right hand—one with a sharp golden point and the other of lead without a point. The lord had two large wings on his shoulders and sat upon two eagles with his feet resting on two lions. To his right knelt a very beautiful lady, resembling Biancofiore. She was praying to the lord humbly, but for what? The words were lost in the noise of a stormy sea to the left of the lord. A rudderless ship with a broken mast and ripped sails was trying to navigate that sea. Florio was on that ship, naked but for a scarf around his eyes. He did not know what to do with the ship. A black spirit emerged from the sea, sized the bow and pulled it down with such force that half of it was submerged in the high waves. Frightened by the power of the spirit and the conditions of the ship, Florio ran toward the stern shouting, "Help" at that lord.

Without moving to help him, the lord spoke. "I am the one you have called so much in time of sorrow. Do not think that I will let you perish. Have faith in me." Still he received no help from this god. When the ship was almost covered with waves, he cried for Jupiter's help.

Almost immediately, a beautiful maiden, completely naked but for a thin veil wrapped around her body, appeared and spoke to him. "Oh, light of my eyes, take comfort."

"What comfort can I take when I am almost under the waves?" cried out Florio.

"Cast away from your ship the evil spirit trying to sink it with its power."

"And how will I do that, since I am unarmed and unclothed?"

From behind the white veil the maiden pulled a flaming sword and gave it to him.

Florio took the sword and felt stronger and safer.

"Since you are the only one helping me, can you please tell me your name? You look familiar, but I am too confused to know you."

"I am your Biancofiore over whom today you have grieved without reason." After that she gave him a branch of green olive and disappeared.

With the burning sword in hand, Florio went very easily over the waves and attacked the evil spirit, wounding it many times. After many blows, the spirit let the ship go and returned to the depths of the sea. Immediately the ship righted itself, the sea waves abated and the storm vanished. As he was about to fix the broken rudder and mast, he woke up. An olive branch was on the bed, next to him. And so was the sword.

The dream was too vivid to discount it outright. He tried to remember it, but only fragments came to his mind. Almost aloud, he began thinking. *Love must have heard my prayers, and maybe it will rekindle in Biancofiore the feelings she had for me. That being the case, I would rather wait for Biancofiore to show me what she wants than kill myself without letting her know what Fileno told me.* With that he put away the sword and sat down to write a letter to Biancofiore, the tenor of which was, "I have loved you from the moment I learned what love was and I have never stopped loving you day and night, near and far, in joyous days and sad ones. I have been faithful to you no matter how many young women, beautiful enough for the gods, have tried to ease my pains with their love and charms. Not one of them could win my heart totally dedicated to serving you. When I heard that you were unjustly condemned to a cruel death, I came to your aid and, with the help of the gods, I fought and pulled you out of danger. I have never regretted anything I felt for you or done for you. Now I hear that you, taken by the deceitful attentions of Fileno, have turned from my love to his in a short time. You cannot deny this because he told me all that himself. He even showed me the veil you gave him. I would have ripped it from his hands if I hadn't so much respect for it.

"Do you not know how many women have asked my father to marry me? And how many others he has proposed for me? I am who and what I am, compared to Fileno, but I also know that fondness makes an ugly villain look beautiful, a worthless one most precious, and the lowest serf very noble. Aside from all that, where is your faithfulness? Where do you hope to find another Florio who loves you as much as I do? I have not erred toward you except in loving you too honestly.

Now you punish me by forsaking me for someone else. If all of that is true, my life will not last much longer, and on my grave, it will be written: 'Here lies Florio dead for loving Biancofiore.'

"If any of this is untrue, do not delay in telling me because as long as I nurse this doubt, I will hold the sword you gave me in my hands, ready to use it or discard it according to what I hear from you. No more for now other than to say: I was yours alive, and yours I will die."

He sealed the letter and gave it to his most trusted servant. "Take this letter to Biancofiore and beg her to give you an answer. If she does, bring it to me immediately, quietly, and earnestly."

The servant followed Florio's order and delivered the missive to Biancofiore. As soon as she saw it, Biancofiore asked how Florio was faring.

The servant replied, "Gracious lady, he is sad and bitter, but I do not know why. He would like a prompt reply to this letter, for which I will wait."

Biancofiore kissed Florio's letter a dozen times before she opened it to read it. But after the first lines she began to cry so much she could hardly see the words. She told the messenger to wait for her and went to her room, where she read the letter many times, stopping often to wipe her tears with handkerchiefs and veils. Eventually still crying, she sat down and wrote to Florio that she had never stopped loving him, that nobody would ever take his place, and that she had given Fileno her veil only to please his mother.

"Besides," she wrote, "perfect love cannot be enclosed in a veil or a jewel. Only the heart can serve that purpose. And I, who feel love for you more than any other, can speak of it with true words. As the gods to whom nothing can be hidden are my witnesses, no person in the world is loved by me, except Florio. Therefore, regard your life dearly as well as mine. At the right time and place the gods will change their minds, granting us a better life than the one we might choose on our own. Do not be idle and melancholic; seek honest pleasures and if you still cherish me in your heart as much as I do you, you know that I am no less worried than you are. I beg you not to disturb my soul with any such letters, for just as you hold my knife in your hands, a short rope would not allow me to endure the reading of a second similar letter. Biancofiore, who was and will always be yours..."

She finished and sealed the letter and gave it to the awaiting messenger. He turned around, jumped on his horse and returned to Florio before dawn. Florio read the letter many times over, thinking on the words of Biancofiore and making various suppositions over them. He lay on the bed for a long time, trying to understand what was happening to the two of them. He did not know what to believe or disbelieve. He wished the gods would help him make such a life-changing decision. He was about to receive their help from an unexpected source.

Chapter Twenty-Two

Diana, the only goddess to whom no sacrifice had been offered when Biancofiore was rescued from the stake, had been furious ever since, and her wrath had grown daily in her heart until now. Unable to hold it any longer without assuaging its rancour, she descended from the divine kingdoms and reached the cold cave of Jealousy in the Appennine Alps. It was completely surrounded by snow, with no vegetation but briars and nettles, no happy birds but cuckoo and owls, and no sign of active life. The windowless enclave was closed by a strong door.

When the goddess touched it with her hand, two dogs began barking furiously and loudly inside the place until an old woman came to the door and asked arrogantly, "Who dares to touch our door?"

"The one without whose help every effort of yours would be lost," said Diana.

The ancient hag slowly opened the door, making such strident noises they could be heard at the foot of the mountain. Having let the goddess pass through, she re-closed the door, barely shielding the goddess's veils from the fangs of the rabid dogs trying to bite her. She chased them away with her raucous voice and the stick she used as a walking cane.

The entire place was covered with soot and spiderwebs. The walls were caked with disgusting mould, and seemed as if they were weeping from sweat. There was no fire to keep the cold out, yet in one of the corners there was a bit of ash in which glowed two cinders already spent, most of which had been taken by a scrawny cat. The old hag seemed to be the perfect resident of the place. Gaunt, smelly, discoloured in her face, her crossed eyes were red and constantly blearing. Dressed in black wraps, she sat on the floor next to the sad fire, all trembling from cold or fear. Her chest was small, its bones protruding under the skin like those of a living corpse. She sat next to the cat, and waited for the goddess to speak.

Diana gave her the mission. "Oh ancient mother, eager repeller of the shameful guiles of Cupid and custodian of our cold fires, you must plant the seed of jealousy into the heart of a young man named Florio, dear to me but hurting me because he loves Biancofiore, an enemy of mine. Go and deprive him of his pure trust in her, convince him that he is deceived, and teach him how to respond to such deceits."

The old woman raised her head, looked at Diana sideways, and answered with trembling whispers. "Goddess of the hunt and the moon, I will do your bid immediately."

Diana smiled at her knowingly and left her.

The old woman changed clothes, added wings to her shoulders, and went to Florio's place. She found him still on his bed, reading Biancofiore's letter again and again.

Invisible to him, but for a cold wind draught coming suddenly through his open window, she secretly touched his concerned heart with her trembling hand and left him.

Feeling a sudden chill, Florio jumped off the bed and went to close the window.

As soon as the old woman touched Florio's inner heart or mind, he began to suspect that he was being played for a fool by Biancofiore. He sat up and started to walk around the room, asking himself questions and responding as if he were an alter ego.

"She definitely deceives me."

"How do you know?"

"She writes out of fear, not out of love."

"Fear of what?"

"Discovery. She does not want me to know that Fileno pleases her more than I do."

"What makes you say that?"

"She took the veil from her head, gave it to him, but she does not love him?"

"Only a simpleton would believe that."

"He is there day and night; you are away all the times. Can you blame her?"

"Not really. A fire is rekindled by soft breezes."

"Love is nourished by sweet deeds."

"A fire dies without air."

"Love dies without care."

"But if she does not love me, why is she saying such sweet things to me?"

"I do not understand that either. Maybe it's a woman's thing."

"She loves me above all things, if I look at the whole picture, right?"

"If she does not love you, Fileno *must* be the reason.

"If that's the case, I *must* avenge myself without any doubt."

"What if Fileno takes her away?"

"I'll pursue him to the ends of the earth."

"What if Fileno asks the king for her hand and he gives her to him?"

"A royal wedding. I would have heard something to that effect."

"Effect? Cause? That's the way to go: Cause and Effect."

"I do not understand. What are you saying?"

"Separation is the cause of why Biancofiore changed her mind about you. Remove the cause and that will remove the effect."

"Do you mean I should go back home and elope with Biancofiore?"

"That's one option. You two can go to some remote place and live without fear."

"And my parents? They surely like to groom Fileno for Biancofiore."

"Then you go to the next option: have Fileno killed or expelled from your town."

"Either choice would eliminate the cause. But I'd still worry about the effect."

"Leave that problem to the gods. It will give them something to do."

Wrecked by violent urgings and bitter reflections, Florio spent most of the time trying desperately to decide which plan to discard and which to adopt. Most miserable among miserable people are those who allow *jealousy* to enter their hearts. Florio was now *possessed* by jealousy. And jealousy dictated that in one way or another Fileno had to go. But the goddess Diana could not let that happen.

Chapter Twenty-Three

As soon as Diana realised that her jealousy weapon had misfired, she ran to Venus for advice. "What crime has Fileno committed for which he deserves death? We can't let that happen simply because he is in love. Because of us this young knight might be harmed."

Venus agreed to a point. "Florio is my follower, but so is Fileno. Love should not be a capital sentence for either one. But you started this by being ridiculously piqued by Florio's grateful offerings to us after we helped him rescue his love. He did not skip you intentionally. But you brought in Jealousy intentionally. Now *you* must stop it. Warn Fileno that he is in imminent danger."

"How can I do that? Unlike you, I do not mingle with mortals," lied Diana.

Venus looked at her contemptuously. "Really? Anyway, warn him by dream. I do it. Often."

Diana did just that.

She went to the House of Sopor, hidden under dark clouds in the cave of a hollowed mountain, which the sun could never penetrate with its rays. It was always night there. The ground produced fog filled with darkness and poppies that contributed to the power of that place. The Lethe River surrounded the house springing from a hard rock and ran over little stones to produce a sweet murmur, which lulled the listener to sleep. There were no birds, no beasts, and no wind. Every branch rested. A silent calm reigned over the place. There was no door to open, no sound to be made, no dog barking, no rooster to announce dawn's arrival. The middle of the great house was occupied by a beautiful bed of feathers, covered entirely with black drapery over which rested Morpheus, the gracious king of sleep, surrounded by dreams waiting to be sent to the people asleep.

The goddess entered the house, constantly putting her hands on her face to chase sleep away. Her arrival in white robes brought enough light into the place to awaken the king. He raised his heavy eyes only enough to ask, "What do you seek here?"

The goddess, fighting to keep her eyes open, spoke between many yawns. "Oh sleep, most pleasant of all things, appeaser of the mind, repeller of anxiety, mitigator of labour, reliever of hardships, equal dispenser of visions, order that Fileno, innocent young man in love, be told in his sleep of the traps set against him so that by knowing about them he might watch out for them."

She finished and hurried out of there, barely able to chase sleep away from her.

The ancient Morpheus awoke his numberless children he had among men, beasts, plants, on land, in water, in the woods and in rocks and in all those forms they can appear as empty shadows in the human minds or in reality. After choosing among them those who seemed more suitable to his needs, he taught them how to fulfil the goddess' wish, and went back to sleep.

Chapter Twenty-Four

That night Fileno had a dream. He was in a green meadow listening to the warbling of birds and admiring the serenity of the place when a dear neighbour—actually one of Morpheus' minions in disguise—came running toward him crying, "Fileno, what are doing here? Get up and run immediately to save your life. Your love for Biancofiore has marked you for death. Prince Florio, with many armed companions, will soon be here to destroy you. You must leave right now."

He had just been warned by his friend when a band of armed men, their faces covered with helmets that made them look even more truculent and frightening, broke into the room screaming, "Death to the traitor! Death to Fileno!" and began to slash at him with such fury and savagery that soon his body could not take much more pain. Fortunately, he awoke at that point to find himself not full of blood, but drenched with sweat. Yet his dream had been realistic enough to make him run out of the house and into that of the neighbour who had warned him in his dream.

The neighbour was very disconcerted by that unexpected visit in the middle of the night, but after he was told of the dream, he sat Fileno down and advised him.

"Thank the gods for that dream. It is a timely warning and a true one. I just came back from a business trip in Montorio where I heard that Florio plans to have you killed because of that veil Biancofiore gave you. If I were you, I'd leave this town immediately."

"Kill me for a veil? Is he jealous of my jousting skills or what?"

"Jealous of anyone even looking at Biancofiore. Didn't you know?"

"Not at all. You know I have been out of the country for a while, but nobody at court said a word about Florio's jealousy. Even his parents encouraged me to woo her."

"Only because they don't want their son involved with her. It's a family rancour."

"Rancour doesn't even begin to describe this. He hates me for loving her; now what would he do if I hated her?"

"Love you," replied his friend without hesitation. "Look, Fileno, I am a business man. But the ways of love are different from the ways of business. In love, no one wants a partner."

"But I would rather die young than live in misery without her," cried Fileno.

"No, you wouldn't," reassured his friend. "We don't know what the future brings. Another day, another friend, another venture, another love."

"But running from a fight is the way of a coward. I am a warrior."

"And what would you do alone against so many? Believe me, to live in any way is better than to die. In life, you can recover everything lost. In death everything ends for you, not for the living. Give life a chance, my friend."

Fileno thought about it for a while, walking the room while his friend nodded sympathetically. Then he turned around to leave.

"I think you are right, after all," admitted Fileno. "I will be on my way. Adieu."

"No," implored his friend. "Let me go with you. Company is what you need at a time like this."

"No, I'd rather grieve alone than depress you with my melancholy. No, you stay here, but if anything changes favourable to my return, send for me quickly wherever the fates might have sent me." Fileno embraced his friend near tears.

"And that is exactly what I will do, Fileno." They hugged with a hardy goodbye.

That same night Fileno left secretly on a self-imposed exile that took him all the way to the hills around Napoli.

Chapter Twenty-Five

But in a royal palace nothing is kept secret for a long time. When the next music recital was held and Fileno did not show up, the king inquired about his whereabouts. A steward told him that the young knight had left town to save his life. Florio's jealousy was behind his escape. The king immediately decided that once again Biancofiore was the cause of it all. She had to be stopped. Another strategy session with the queen was in order. He called for her. She came to his room quickly and listened attentively as the king rambled on.

"I do not know what course to take... All my hopes and plans are wrapped around the finger of a little whore... She has bewitched him with some herbs or magic... I've never heard of a woman lingering this long in a man's mind, let alone a boy's... But I will change that... I'll make my own magic... with my sword in her eager bosom... The fates will not save her this time... I will do it..."

The queen smiled at him in the condescending way of someone who knows better. "May the gods forbid that a king's hands be tainted with the death of a simple girl. We have a thousand servants who can do that. No,

I have a better way. Bloodless. Guiltless. Effortless."

The king stopped raving. "No blood? No guilt? No struggle?"

The queen shook her head at each rhetorical question. Then she explained.

"I've been meaning to talk to you about it several times, but since the situation has arisen, I'll do it now. A few days ago, I heard that an Egyptian ship has anchored in our Mallorca port with a rich cargo. Once the cargo has been unloaded it will depart. Summon the ship's owners and sell Biancofiore to them. I am sure they will love to take a blonde beauty to their far-away shores, and no one will ever hear of her again."

"What about our son? What will we tell him?"

"We'll tell Florio that she died suddenly. There is always a plague going around."

"We must give her a royal burial, of course."

"Of course. I'll take care of the details. And then we will be rid of this annoyance once and for all."

"Don't you think Florio will be terribly upset by her… disappearance?"

"Florio is young, handsome, learned and a future king. He will have no trouble finding a replacement for Biancofiore."

Extremely pleased with the plan, the king immediately summoned two knights to contact the ship owners and find out from them the ship's origin, nature of the cargo, and departure date. One more thing: would they be interested in buying the most beautiful slave in the world?

The knights carried out the king's orders and came back with the information he needed. The ship belonged to Menone and Antonio from Alexandria. It carried spices, pearls, gold, and Indian fabrics. It would be reloaded with local products and return to Egypt soon after that. The owners also promised to wait for any length of time needed to do the king's pleasure. And yes, they would buy such a slave if she was as beautiful as they said she was. In fact, they would come on the following day with the treasure needed to acquire such a girl.

Chapter Twenty-Six

Two days later, having loaded their sacks of emeralds and gold coins, the two merchants came to Marmorina and were warmly received by the king. To them he explained the reason for the transaction.

"This young lady committed an outrageous crime against the crown. However, she is so young and so beautiful that I just cannot take her life as demanded by our laws. But just so her crime does not remain unpunished, I will sell her to the highest bidder. Are you interested?"

The merchants opened their coffers to show their splendid contents. "If she is as beautiful as reported, there is enough here to buy one hundred pretty maidens from your majesty."

The king calmly replied, "See for yourselves, gentlemen." He then turned to the queen. "Go and bring out the young maiden."

At his command, the queen went to her room where Biancofiore sat embroidering a kerchief. Gesticulating excitedly the queen announced, "Great news, Biancofiore. Florio is on his way here. Dress yourself elegantly so he will see you are as beautiful as ever."

When she heard those words, Biancofiore almost fainted from joy, but with the help of the queen she prepared herself to meet Florio. Rushing from closet to trunks, she slipped into a silver-laced dress that tightly embraced her body, rolled her golden hair up high like a Greek goddess, put a coronet on her head, and almost ran out of the room to look for her beloved Florio from the palace window.

The queen stopped her and guided her to the great hall. Biancofiore followed her as if in a daze. When the queen stopped, Biancofiore looked, but instead of Florio she saw two strange merchants surrounded by coffers overflowing with coins and jewels and staring at her as if she were Venus.

Completely transfixed by her beauty, the merchants could barely speak. So they leaned closer to the king and whispered to him, "Lord, take from our treasures any amount you like for this priceless pearl."

The king agreed ominously.

Biancofiore was stupefied. She kept looking at the merchants and the king and queen, unable to grasp the sense or meaning of the situation. The king saw her distraction and addressed it.

"Dear Biancofiore, remember the pledge I made on my birthday? Well, I am keeping it right now. I have married you to Sardano, Lord of Carthage, and a dear relative of ours. He awaits you with a great feast, as the present gentlemen who have come to take you there have told us. You will go with them, but I will forever be your father, if your bloodline is ever questioned."

As soon as she heard those words, Biancofiore felt her blood leaving her face and a coldness coming into her heart. Still she managed to remain strong enough to respond.

"Sweet lord, I would obey you, but I can't be married because when thrown in a dark dungeon, I made a vow of eternal chastity to Diana, if she would rescue me. She did, and I must keep my vow."

"How can your beauty expect a life of virginity when it is obviously moulded for... for loving?" babbled the king.

"Besides," quickly added the queen perturbed by the king's awkwardness, "our mother Juno, goddess of Matrimony, will release you from that vow as soon as you are officially wedded."

"I fear that Diana will be justly angered and vindictive toward me," opined Biancofiore.

"She will not be, I assure you," insisted the king with an edge of impatience in his voice. And even so, the deal is made and cannot be undone." He turned to the queen for approval.

The queen peevishly added, "Silly girl, you should have told us of your vow when you first made it."

Biancofiore was becoming desperate for a way out.

"But, my queen, it is for ladies to bring a dowry to the husband, not to receive it; and to go to him with great fanfare, not alone; and for wedding ambassadors to dress formally, not like gaudy merchants whispering who knows what," she complained.

"All of that is unimportant," ruled the king. "But I will allow you to keep Gloritia, your mother's maid, as your travel companion. Nothing else. Now go with these gentlemen and heed their orders because they are my orders." And he left the hall.

Biancofiore was semiconscious when the merchants gently took her off the queen's arms and brought her and Gloritia to their ship.

That same day the ship sailed toward distant shores.

Chapter Twenty-Seven

The ship was rolling over the agitated waters of the Mediterranean Sea when Biancofiore woke up from a sleep or a fainting—she was not sure which. Looking around from the porthole in her cabin, she could see and hear the waves crashing against the hull. Gloritia was at her side when she began crying in a most pitiful way about her condition.

"Oh Gloritia, what have I done to be abandoned by my gods and my love? And why am I again in a dismal situation? I know I am a slave now. These merchants paid money for me. And where am I really going? Who will ever know what happened to me?"

She cried so loudly and so long that Gloritia sent a cabin boy to call the merchants below deck.

They came immediately and raised Biancofiore off Gloritia's lap and took her in their arms not like a slave, but like a dear sister. They sprinkled some scented water on her face to calm her down and took turns speaking to her.

"Oh, most beautiful young lady, why are you so unhappy?"

"You are not sad because you left that old king who

wanted to end your life?"

"You should be happy for that."

"We paid a fortune for you, but do not ever think of yourself as a slave, ever."

"We will honour you as a lady in every respect. We swear by your gods."

"Is it because you miss the place you lived in? Fear not; we are going to an even better place, full of beautiful things and pleasant people."

"Sometimes the places that seem perfect for our plans are the ones that will ruin our best-laid plans."

"But look at you: you are rich, gracious, and very beautiful. You must be one of the gods' favourites."

"Smile, Misery cannot last long with you. Let those without hope weep for their misfortune."

Biancofiore listened to their words and saw some truth in them. She stopped crying, much to the relief of Gloritia and then she said, "I thank you for your comforting me. I feel a little better already knowing that you two are caring people."

The merchants left her to go back on the ship's deck and tend to their sailing.

Then Biancofiore raised her hands to the sky and prayed to her gods.

"Venus, goddess of love, who helped me in the darkness of that dungeon, keep me safe company. Without you I go without hope. And I also pray to you, chaste Diana. I am still one of your virgins and will be until my nuptials. Concede that I may preserve your benefits intact for my Florio. If the fates do not allow him to receive them, kill me first before they are taken from me."

And with that, a sweet sleep finally came to her, and the words and the tears ended at the same time. Gloritia covered her with a soft linen blanket and then sat on the floor next to her in vigil.

And the goddesses Biancofiore had prayed to appeared to her in her dream.

Diana, dressed in her hunting costume, spoke to her first. "Sad Biancofiore, although you and Florio forgot me when you offered sacrifices to the other gods for your rescue, I am ready to forgive you because the great adversities you endured have washed away my anger. I promise that your wish will be granted. No one will rob you of what you vowed to keep for Florio."

Then spoke Venus, shining with fiery light, her nakedness wrapped in a purple veil.

"My dear and faithful subject, stop crying and start facing adversities with more optimism. Your prayers have earned our pledge that Florio will search for you and find you in the most unimaginable place in the world."

After those words, both goddesses disappeared, and Biancofiore woke. She immediately told Gloritia about the dream. Together they prayed that their journey would come to a happy ending. But it would take some doing, even with the gods' help.

And it was with the help of Neptune, calming the waves that the ship sailed through in the blue Mediterranean, stopping briefly in Rhodes to buy some supplies and to rest the crew, and continuing without any major setback into the port of Alexandria.

Here they were received most amiably by the noble Darius the Alexandrian and by the admiral of the powerful king of Babylon who governed that city. To him the merchants brought Biancofiore and their account of her ordeal and subsequent sale for a large sum of coins.

When the admiral saw her, he told the merchants to name their own price for the very beautiful maiden and to the assembled retinue he said, "I swear by my gods that Fortune will not be able to be against her any more. In fact, next month, when my king will come to visit here, I will give her to him in gratitude for his generosity to me. But I promise to all of you that she will be the foremost among his wives. To that intent, she will wear the ancient crown of Queen Semiramis, whose name means 'Gift from the Sea', as a most fitting homage for Biancofiore, a gift from our sea. Hence, she will be honoured among all women kept for a similar purpose under diligent guard in the Tower of the Arab, and provided with all the necessities and delights due to a lady of her rank."

The merchants were extremely happy for the

outcome of their transaction not only because they made so much money, but also because they could see a happy turnaround for Biancofiore.

But she was not so happy, being in a strange land among strange people, with strange customs. Yet she had faith in the goddess's words and waited patiently for the fulfilment of their promise.

Chapter Twenty-Eight

Back in Marmorina, the king was not waiting for the gods' intervention into his affairs. Realising that the absence of Biancofiore would soon be noticed by the court gadflies and reported to Florio, he decided to let people believe that she was dead. Who knew, maybe that would convince Florio to look at other maidens for company and solace. With that in mind, he summoned several trusty craftsmen and ordered them to quickly build a beautiful tomb of carved marble right next to that of Julia, Biancofiore's mother. When the place was ready, he took the body of a young woman who had died the night before, dressed her in Biancofiore's best clothes and had her buried in the marbled tomb while hired mourners lamented her death.

Everyone believed the story that he spread—except those he had paid for their labour and their silence. He then sent a courier to Florio with this message: "If you like to see Biancofiore before she leaves this life, you must come immediately to Marmorina. A serious illness has suddenly seized her and might kill her at any moment."

When Florio first heard the news, he went crazy

with sorrow and anger. He took his sword and started slashing at furniture, bedpost, cabinets and library shelves as if he were attacking a hoard of enemies. But after a while, as his tutor Ascaleon and others calmed him down, his wild outbreak became a cynical and more controlled anger of disbelief, as he asked to no one in particular, "How can a healthy, active young woman die so suddenly? Was I not told that she was sick? Did she fall off the castle ramparts? Was she bitten by a viper? Or was she brought down by my conniving parents? I must know. I need to find the truth."

When those around him agreed that it was a very strange and most suspicious story, he had his war horse readied and asked his good friends to be his armed escort. In a matter of hours, he was galloping with them toward Marmorina.

When he reached the royal palace, he entered it with his retinue, ran up the stairs with his horse before dismounting in front of his mother, who met him outside the great hall.

"Where is Biancofiore? What happened to her?" he asked her.

Without answering, the queen embraced him and began to sob uncontrollably while leading him into the hall. There was the king, dressed in purple mourning clothes, sitting on the throne, surrounded by many courtiers. The king stood up quickly, came down, embraced him, and kissed him on both cheeks several times. Florio did not respond with kisses as customary. The king spoke to him, but also to the assemblage.

"Dear son, it would have pleased me very much if you had returned sooner to see life in one whose death now you must endure with patience. The gods, envious of so much beauty and goodness, had her climb up to their place. She is happy in the new world, but we feel the anguish of her absence, since we loved her for her virtues and for the love you bore for her. But take comfort. The gods that took her will give you one even prettier and nobler to console you. She has left the world's cares; do not give her new pains with your sorrow. It is doubly sinful to disrespect those who are beatified after their death."

Florio could not endure the hypocrisy of his father any longer. He rendered his garments and began to scream in anger, sorrow, and disbelief.

"Oh, heartless man, why didn't you kill me instead? What had that young girl done to deserve death from you or your ministers? Do you think that flattering words can heal the wound made by your bitter knife? Only death can do that. So, now you are happy. You have what you wanted the most in your life. But I swear I will make you grieve for such joy."

Then unable to control his emotion, he began weeping unashamedly and ran to his old room where he spent the night thinking of Biancofiore and of the happy days they spent together. But such remembrances did not bring him any relief nor needed sleep. Instead they intensified his pain and his anger. He felt and looked miserable.

At the first light of the next day, Florio went to his mother's room and asked her to take him to Biancofiore's tomb. She reacted with regal indignity.

"What? Visit her tomb in such a condition? Look at you; people will think that you are out of your mind to mourn so outrageously a plebeian maiden like Biancofiore! There are so many princesses just waiting to marry you. For one, the daughter of the king of Granada could soon be your bride if you behave like a prince."

"Mother, do not try to comfort with empty words the sadness you have caused with deceit. Only a fool takes as healer the enemy from whom he has just been wounded. Let me see where lies the one you have killed and whom I will join today."

The queen realised that her approach was useless and unwelcome. So she agreed to walk him toward the tomb of Biancofiore. Many people followed them, all of them wailing dramatically for Florio and his lost maiden, rending their clothes in sympathy, and grieving with each other as they followed their queen and her son.

When they reached the tomb, Florio embraced it as if it could bring its content back to life and cried most unhappily and inconsolably. That created louder outcries from the lamenting crowd that now felt sorrier for Florio than it would have for Biancofiore. Florio himself began to talk almost in a lugubrious sing-song fashion of their love.

Moments of happiness, games played, songs sung, books read, smiles and tears, pranks and secret mockeries, longings felt but repressed, dreams and traumas: they all came back to him, like a montage of tableaux vivants that would be indelibly etched in his memory.

And he concluded, "I was the cause of your death, poor Biancofiore. To obey my enemy I have lost you, my sweetest friend. The gods, Fortune, my parents—all envied our love and caused your death. But that love will lead me to you, even today."

As he said that, he rose from the tomb, drew out his sword and was about to plunge it into his chest when his mother grabbed his arm with a very loud scream.

"Don't do it, Florio. Don't kill yourself for one who still lives."

Was it the great uproar that arose above the screaming and weeping? Was it the shock of the revelation that did not quickly register with Florio? Was it the strength of his mother, now aided by others, that stopped his fatal thrust? Florio was obviously unaware of the news, as he kept asking, "Why do you stop me, Mother? My death might be delayed, but not avoided. I want it to take me here, by my Biancofiore."

"Dear son, why do you want to punish your father, me, and the whole kingdom with this useless act? I told you: Biancofiore lives."

A murmur ran through the crowd, as more people heard the news. Yet Florio was unconvinced.

"Mother, your words deceive me no more. Your lies will not prolong my life."

"We lied about her being dead. But I am not lying about her being alive."

"How can I believe someone who lied to me before?"

"Just look at the proof. Open the tomb. This is no Biancofiore."

He did just that. His mother was right. The only Biancofiore thing was the dress worn by another dead woman.

"So where is she?" asked Florio with a mixture of comfort and puzzlement.

"She is not here. Where she is... let us go to the palace. I will tell you there."

"Is this another trick to keep me alive? It won't work, I can assure you."

"I know, but trust me. Put that sword away. I will tell you all at the palace."

And she did, omitting nothing, expressing no sorrow, still believing it was all done for Florio's good, for the royal heir's good, and for the Spanish kingdom's good.

Florio was neither impressed nor convinced. If anything, the account of his parents' perfidy hardened his will to resist their entreaties to remain at the court and look for a future queen among the many nubile ladies that adored him.

In the harshest, and coldest manner he had ever addressed them, he said, "If I were born of lions or tigers, my parents would be more caring than you. For the pains you have inflicted on me, I should have you killed. But I do not want your vile blood on my hands. I'll let the gods take care of that, and may they have no mercy on you."

His remarks struck deeply into his mother's heart. Amidst flowing tears, she said, "Your words are not surprising since you speak them in anger. But remember this: no creature loves you as much as I and your father do. We did what we did to make your life more glorious than it will be now. But this much is clear now: the god of those innocent pilgrims attacked by your father has not let such tort remain unpunished. And my wish that the damned baby girl I carried in my arms would always be your companion has also come true—much to my regret."

After that, she covered her head with a shawl and walked away silently. The king gave Florio one last glare, and followed the queen.

Chapter Twenty-Nine

Florio left his parents to their sorrows and regrets, but summoned his knights and friends, including Ascaleon, Parmenion, Menedon and Messaallino, and spoke to them in the great hall.

"I have summoned you, as the dearest to me, to take up with me voluntary exile from here, and I beseech you especially, old Ascaleon, to be a father, teacher, and guide to us, for we are all young and no one has ever gone out of our country into unknown places. We will religiously follow your steps like sons. My mission, to find Biancofiore, I believe pleases the gods so that my young years will not be wasted in laziness. Those of you who are as young as I heed my plea and whoever of you as a faithful friend wishes to serve me freely answer *yes,* without trying to show me that my undertaking is shallow or useless. I know what I am doing and no one could convince me to do otherwise."

Ascaleon answered for himself, but probably for everyone else when he said, "I well know how love compels: therefore, let any cause move you. I, as a guide and as a vassal, will follow you to the golden sands of the Indian Ganges, through the rough waters of the Don, through the white kingdoms of the powerful Boras and the arid regions of Libya, and even to any other hemisphere unseen by men. No, even if you descend into the dark kingdom of Dis, or if there is a way to fly to the abodes of the celestial gods, we will seek them with you, and you will never be deserted as long as there is life in me."

The others applauded in agreement, shouting, "*Pro patria mori*." They were ready to go. But Florio was not.

Chapter Thirty

Florio had to take a formal leave from his parents. So he went to his father and told him, "Since you thought more of pearls and gold than of my love, I must go and find her wherever she might be. But as your son and a follower of the knights' code, I must ask for your consent to leave."

"What are you asking me, to give up the only son I have? The kingdom is yours for the taking; what else can I give you? Here, take all the gold paid for Biancofiore. Send others to search for her or leave after I die, but not now, not like this," pleaded his father.

"I will take the gold because I might need it to rescue her, but I will leave with or without your permission. If you had learned anything from the past experiences, you'd know that I loved her so much I would follow her wherever you might have sent her, which is one more reason for coming here. Where did those merchants come from?"

The king replied almost in tears. "In the past I tried to oppose the gods' will and suffered badly for my actions. I will not do so now. The merchants went back to Alexandria. You might start your search there. If you find her, come back immediately for I will never be happy until I see you again."

It was his mother's turn to bid him goodbye. She did so with her face drenched with tears.

"Son, since neither prayer nor pity can keep you here, take this ring and carry it with you to remember your wretched mother. It is a special ring from Iarbas, king of the Gaetulains, our ancestors. And it has miraculous powers: it will make you likable to all people, quench the hot flames of Vulcan, and save you from the cold waters of Neptune. Until your safe return home, I'll pray to the gods to guard over you and save you from evil people."

Florio took the ring and left without embracing either parent. As he was leaving the palace, he was met by Ferramonte, the duke of Montorio, who had heard of Florio's expedition. The duke was adamant about his participation at any cost. Florio thanked him very much for his loyalty and friendship, asking him to be ready to go on the next day. But first, he had an announcement to make to the five leaders of the group. For that they went to a mead hall where he told them, "Dear friends, the whole world knows of my father's power and my bloodline to him. Now, we don't know exactly where Biancofiore is and who is holding her captive. When we get in that area, her captors hearing of my arrival might kill her or keep her hidden until we leave. Therefore, to avoid such dire consequences, you should call me by another name, and the one I have chosen is *Filocolo*."

"*Filocolo*?" asked everyone. "We have never heard such a name. What is it?"

"As my teacher Ascaleon could tell you, it comes from two Greek words: philos, meaning love, and colon meaning labour. So, FILOCOLO means LABOR OF LOVE, which defines what this expedition is all about. The arrival of Prince Florio would make news in most places; the arrival of someone called Filocolo will stir no interest among the people or the authorities of any place. Like you, they will say, "Filocolo? Never heard of him."

Ascaleon spoke for the group. "I would have never guessed that my Greek lessons would be put to such usage, but we are in full agreement with you. Filocolo you will be until this labour is completed and your quest fulfilled. May the gods speed us in that direction."

Unfortunately for them, or maybe fortunately by the will of the gods, their plan would be changed the very next day when they were about to board their ship. The river, greatly engorged with run-off waters, had become too dangerous to board with a full cargo, let alone navigate with horses and people. After a short consultation with the sailors, they decided to send the ship downriver and meet it at Pisa on the Adige River, while they moved south on horseback. Their travels and travails had just begun.

Chapter Thirty-One

The caravan moved slowly along the riverbanks, fully aware of the possibility of sudden floods. After they left the clear waves of the Secchia, climbed the forested shoulders of the Apennines, they descended them and came by the Arno River near the ancient walls of Florence. Here they decided to take not the straight road to Alphea, but one safer if a bit longer and arrived in the lonely plain, near the robust fir forest into which, unbeknown to them, had fled the wretched Fileno. Again, circling around flooded lands, they spotted from far away some ancient but inviting walls, where there could be places for resting and taking care of the horses. When they reached them, they realised that this must have been a temple of ancient gods.

Filocolo decided that since the gods had brought them here, he should offer sacrifices to unknown and strange gods, mindful of not offending any deity. Having removed the weeds, bushes and brambles, which had grown upon the old altar, he then cleaned the statues of the old gods and adorned them with fresh ornaments, and had fragrant fires lit upon the altar. He then ordered that a bull be brought forward.

Dressed in proper vestments, he killed the bull with his own hands and offered its entrails into the burning fire as a sacrifice. He then knelt before the altar and prayed devotedly.

"Most high gods, if any of you reside in this deserted place, accept this rough sacrifice made by inexpert but sincere hands. I pray that with the lighted fires and gifts I may deserve some advice from you on my future journey and, with it, help in my labour."

He had just finished the prayer when he heard a great murmur through the temple sweep like pebbles in a swift stream, which after a while became a voice that spoke these words.

"Since you rewarmed our cold altars with devout fires and prayers, we will respond. Tomorrow after you leave this place, you will come to Alphea; there the ship awaits you and on it, after great obstacles, you will reach the Island of Fire where you shall find news of the one you are seeking. Then, departing from there, after many incidents you will reach the place where dwells the one you seek. There, with great danger but no mortal harm, you shall possess the desired object."

The holy voice was silent after that. Filocolo, filled with happiness and wonder, returned to his companions and told them what the voice had predicted. Happy and still wondering, they sat down to eat some food in that wild place. After the meal, Filocolo wandered out into the meadow with an empty cup in his hand to look at the scenery.

It was there that he saw a beautiful natural fountain, gurgling with clear water in spite of the recent rains. He approached it to drink from it and noticed that in the middle the water rose to form two bubbles. He knelt by the spring and agitated the water to fill the cup. While doing this he saw those bubbles swell and between them he heard what began as a gurgle, but soon turned into a human voice.

"Let it suffice that I, who was once a man am now a fountain, can quench your thirst without your stirring my parts unnecessarily."

At the sound of the voice, Filocolo jumped back and almost fell from the shock. His friends came out to see what was happening and they too were full of wonderment and unspoken questions. Filocolo felt the same way, but found enough courage to ask,

"Whoever you are who dwell in these waters, forgive me if I offended or disturbed you accidentally. But if you can, we would like to hear who you are and how you came to be in this place and in this form, so we may tell your story to the people and stir pity in their hearts, if your case deserves pity."

After a brief silence, the waves began to move again and a voice issued from the vicinity of the two bubbles.

"I don't know who you are, but you sound caring and sincere. So, I will tell you. I was from Marmorina, a land of noble people ruled by King Felix of Spain. My name was Fileno. As a young knight visiting the king, I met Biancofiore, the most beautiful girl in the world, and fell in love with her. For one of my jousts I asked for and received from her a head veil to be my fighting colours and bring me luck, which it did as I won the tournament. Later I met the king's son, Florio, to whom I confided my love for Biancofiore, unaware that he loved her most of all. As a result, he began to hate me and planned to kill me. When Diana warned me of such danger in a dream, I escaped from Marmorina and wandered around until I found this place.

"Only in this solitude I could weep over Biancofiore at length and undisturbed. Every day I prayed the gods to end my sorrow and one day, they heard my plea. As I was sitting crying in this spot, a profuse sweat came over me and covered me completely. When I tried to wipe off that sweat, every part I touched turned into water until I felt no more nor less like a wave in the sea.

"Then I realised that my whole person was turning into fluids and felt myself take over this place. Only my mind and my voice were left to me by the gods. The two bubbles you see were my eyes, the source of my constant tears and of this fountain's clear water.

"That thin layer of grass which covers the clear water in some spots was Biancofiore's veil with which I had covered myself the day I was changed into a spring. Now, if you don't mind, would you reveal to me the person to whom I revealed myself?"

When the entourage heard that last request, all faces turned to Filocolo to see and hear his response. They were surprised to see him moved to tears by Fileno's account and waited for his answer. It came amidst his efforts to control his emotion.

"I am called Filocolo and I came from a town very close to your country. I too am wandering through the world filled with bitter pain for being in love. I also know that the Florio you mentioned grieves because his father sold Biancofiore to foreign merchants. Therefore, if he wanted to harm you, the gods have well repaid him for such an offence. Since you are not alone in this predicament, let us hope that Diana will someday reinstate you to your original shape by going into her service."

The clear fountain swelled itself at the end of Filocolo's words, producing new gurglings, but spoke no more. After waiting for some time in silence, they went back into the temple commenting on the strange happening they had just witnessed and wondering what to do.

Chapter Thirty-Two

Filocolo acknowledged their concerns. "It is very clear that the gods sent us here and I wouldn't have missed this wonderous happening for nothing. But I do not know how I can honour this place more than what I have done by renovating the holy temple and its altar."

His friends looked at each other, shaking their heads and opening their arms to signify that nothing more was needed or could be done at that moment. But Ascaleon had an idea.

"We will proceed according to the gods' advice, but when we have completed our journey and achieved our goal, we shall return here to show how grateful we are for the advice received and honour these deities accordingly."

Everyone liked Ascaleon's suggestion and gathered all their equipment to continue their journey toward the port. In time they reached it and found the ship waiting for them. Happy about that, the retinue climbed aboard without delay and gave the red sails to the winds. Soon they were in the middle of the sea with the course of the ship set for the Island of Fire.

The voyage proceeded well for three days,

favourable winds pushing the ship fast over the Mediterranean waves and bringing it very close to the place where they had decided to rest and resupply. But that soon changed when the winds came from all directions, indeed almost in a circular fashion, and rain began to fall incessantly upon the ship. As the sailors tried to keep it straight on the course set by the captain, more winds, lightning, and waves hit the ship. It was one of the most violent storms the veteran sailors had ever encountered. Soon the sails were down, the mast was broken, and one of the two rudders was taken out by the waves. The sky seemed to open itself up. With harsh thunders and repeated lightnings striking the ship, waves running over the decks had sent all her sidings into the sea. By sheer luck they did not lose any passenger or crew as the ship sailed, carried by powerful winds without any steering, before it was hurled eventually into the port of Napoli. Here, finally, damaged on the sides and smashed almost near final destruction, the ship was fastened in a safe place with anchors and everyone climbed on small boats to go on land.

Once in town, they were joyously received by a friend of Ascaleon, who made all the arrangements for repairing the ship and refurbishing it with sails, mast, and rudders better than the original ones. Still they had to wait for good weather to sail out of the bay of Napoli.

But the weather did not improve as rapidly as

Filocolo would have liked or as much as the sailors deemed necessary to resume the voyage. The long delay caused Filocolo to fall into melancholic moods, which he tried to chase away with walks along the seashores, which immediately evoked thoughts of Biancofiore being somewhere across the sea, in unimaginable discomfort and deprivation. That did nothing but increase Filocolo's unhappiness and frustration, in spite of his friends' words of comfort and the many amenities surrounding them.

One of those amenities consisted of meeting congenial people at gatherings hosted by Ascaleon's friend, among whom was a beautiful lady known as Fiammetta. The meetings took the form of anecdotal sparring, all dealing with questions about love. Each participant told a story that buttressed the opinion of the narrator. Fiammetta was the queen of the group and Ascaleon was the moderator of the questions, judging who outwitted the other in this battle-of-the-sexes kind of jousting. Thirteen questions of love were discussed and illustrated by farcical or moralistic tales. By then Filocolo had decided that it was time to leave the jovial group and resume the quest. With weather now offering gentle breezes, they left Napoli on the following day and headed for the Island of Fire, sometimes known as Sicily.

They looked for Biancofiore all over the island, but found none who knew of such a girl. Desperate for any lead to her whereabouts, Filocolo and his companions kept roaming the port cities and villages so much that they attracted the attention of a lady known as Sisife, who finally approached them and asked them in a mannerly fashion whom they were seeking.

"A beautiful, blonde young lady from the land of Spain, who is travelling in the company of two Egyptian merchants," answered Filocolo.

Sisife's eyes dilated first in surprise and then squinted with a bit of suspicion as she inquired with a smile, "But what makes you think that she might be around here?"

"Some ancient god that I honoured told me that I should hear true news of her here. But I find this to be false because I have been here for several days and found no one who has news of her. I begin to think that I was deceived by the gods and I despair I will ever find her," answered Filocolo with a melancholy face to accompany his words.

Sisife then smiled and, much to his surprise, embraced Filocolo like a mother, much to his surprise.

"Young man, you must never lose faith in the gods' promises because they are infallible. The lady you seek is one called Biancofiore. She was my guest for several days some six months ago, when my two relatives stopped here to replenish their ship's supplies. She cried for most of the time over a young man named Florio, whom she loved above all other men in the world."

The news revived Filocolo's spirits and brought a great smile over his face, as he embraced Sisife and kissed her cheeks like an old relative.

"That is the very one I am seeking. She is my sister, and I know that Florio very well, and indeed he loves her as much as she loves him, maybe more. But pray tell me, where could she be now? I will pay those merchants twice their highest price if I can find them and buy her back from them."

"My relatives told me they would stop in Rhodes before they headed for Alexandria, weather permitting and the gods willing. If you find them, entreat them on my behalf about your need. They will be very accommodating to you. If you succeed, and pass by here, I would like to see her again. I grew very fond of her in those few days."

Filocolo rejoiced at the news and promised to stop by and see her again. Grateful for her confirmation of the gods' promise, he gave her several gifts suitable for such a lady before he departed from her with a little more happiness in his heart.

Then they boarded their waiting ship and headed toward the island of Rhodes. On the way there they stopped at several islands, including Crava, Venedigo, Cetri, Sechilo and Pondico. Then on to Candia, Caposermon, Casso, Scarpanto and Trachilo, before finally anchoring into the port of Rhodes. As they left the ship to scout the town, they met, quite by chance,

Bellisano, a local nobleman who had resided in Rome with Ascaleon when they were both training to be knights.

The encounter was fortuitous and enjoyable for both of them, but soon the inevitable question was asked. "What brought you here with such great company?"

Ascaleon told him about Filocolo's search for Biancofiore.

When he heard that, Bellisano was obviously shocked by the coincidence.

"Almost six months ago Biancofiore was in this house with the Ausonian merchants who were bringing her to Alexandria to sell her to the admiral. But I never found out who she was exactly and how she came to be in such a predicament."

Ascaleon told him, "This is the daughter of Lelio Africanus, who was so kind to us while we trained in Rome and who was killed by King Felix when mistaken for a warring party."

Hearing this, Bellisano could barely hold back his tears.

"Oh, dear gods. In my house was the daughter of the man I owe so much to, and I did not give her any help? Had I known that, I would have given those merchants every piece of gold I have to buy her freedom and take her back to Rome. How sad that she told me so much about herself, except her identity."

"We believe you would have," reassured Ascaleon. "But now you can still help by telling us how to find her and rescue her."

"Tell you? No, dear friend. I must come with you. I have some good friends in Alexandria who can be extremely helpful to us," stated Bellisano with firmness.

"Dearest Bellisano, it will suffice to send us to your friends, without exerting yourself." Filocolo tried to dissuade him. "It's a long trip and, with all due respect, you are carrying quite a few years on your back. You need rest more than hardship, but I thank you for your offer."

"It's not a matter of age. My honour and gratitude are at stake. I will risk my life, if need be, for the daughter of a man who did so much for me. I beg you to let me go with you. I can assure you I can do more hard labours than many young men half my age."

Filocolo could not refuse such a plea. He smiled his approval.

"I am sure you can, sir. So, lead us. We will leave when you deem it right."

And they did when Bellisano assured them that the trade winds were just right for the crossing to Alexandria. They reached that glorious city without any trouble or course changes. Once there, Bellisano guided them to the house of Dario, who welcomed them with extreme courtesy and generosity. In fact, according to the local custom, they transacted no business for the first three days of their stay, Dario insisting on dining and feasting and touring the guests through the city squares, passageways, libraries, and ancient walls, much to the chagrin of Filocolo whose mind was not on the scenery of the place, but on the location of his love.

Finally, on the fourth day, Bellisano asked Dario to meet with them and discuss some matters that were at the heart of their visit. When they were all ensconced on thick pillows, around a table filled with delicacies and drinks, Bellisano spoke to Dario.

"We are here on a delicate matter in which you became involved some six months ago. This young man here is the son of the king of Spain, and these are his noble friends. He is looking for a beautiful girl named Biancofiore, brought here by Antonio and his merchant partner. He loves her madly and has vowed to never return to his royal house without her. And we are here to see it happen, with your help. We would be grateful for life if you could tell us anything about her or what we must do, according to your judgement, in order to gain her freedom."

Chapter Thirty-Three

Upon hearing those words, Dario stood up to inspect the room, checking behind every door and column, and chasing away any servant or steward he found in the area. He then returned to the group, gathered them closer to him, and began to whisper to them.

"As most of you know, our ruler, the admiral, is the vassal of the very fussy sultan of Babylon to whom he must deliver an annual tribute of gold and one hundred virgins. To remain in the good grace of the sultan, the admiral will scout even the most remote places of the world to find the most beautiful and noble virgins. Cost is not a factor for his treasury is boundless. Once he finds them, he keeps them in that tower you see across the bridge."

He pointed to a huge tower overlooking an expansive meadow.

"It is the most secure and luxurious construction in Egypt. It has precious columns of porphyry, windows of marble and gold, tapestries of the finest quality and artistry, altars for every god, paintings of every ancestor, and a hundred-room penthouse for the virgins, with ceilings of gold encrusted with sapphires, emeralds, and rubies. The centrepiece of those lodgings is the abode where Biancofiore sleeps—a chamber that surpasses all others in splendour, comfort, and beauty, the place reserved only for the most beautiful among the residents.

"At the summit of the tower there is a stupendous garden in which grows every imaginable bush or flower, irrigated by a marvellous fountain. Just above the fountain grows a magic tree that never loses a leaf because, people say, it was planted by Diana and Ceres. Any time the admiral wants to have proof of a maiden's virginity, he takes her under that tree and watches her. If she is a virgin, a flower falls upon her head and the fountain's water flows quietly and clearly. If she has been with a man already, the flower does not fall and the water becomes turbulent and cloudy. In this manner he has already discovered many women who, being no longer virgin, were cast out from the tower with shameful shouts and vituperations.

"In this garden the maidens sing, dance, play games, and tell stories to enjoy themselves. Actually, they are free to roam throughout the entire tower down to the first floor. From there they cannot go down or out ever without the admiral's permission. And they are watched and tended in every need by men who have one thing in common: they are all eunuchs. And chief among them is an Arab castellan named Sadoc who must think of all the things that are necessary to the

159

virgins and provide them in a timely fashion. But most of all he must guard them day and night.

To help him in this task he has many sergeants. Their number can be seen at sunset when they gather in the meadow around the tower and stand guard with bows and arrows at the ready. No person can even approach the meadow, under the risk of life and limb, without Sadoc's permission.

"That being the situation and Biancofiore's predicament, I can offer but three possible remedies. One, we pray, beg, and implore the admiral to return her to us. Two, we abduct her from the tower by force. Three, we gain the castellan's friendship by trickery and then get her out. The first two options are useless. The admiral will *never* release her, and we could never survive an attack on the tower unless we had Caesar's legions doing the fighting for us. The tower is impregnable. The last option is the only possible one, unless you can think of a better one."

Filocolo looked around for a consensus or different opinions, but he neither saw nor heard any. So he asked Dario, "How can we become friendly with a truculent Arab who gave up his manhood to be a guardian of virgins and will clearly not take kindly to any foreign approach?"

"I'll tell you how," replied Dario immediately. "He is an old, arrogant, miserly chess player who delights in defeating and degrading anyone who challenges him to a chess match. By acting humbly and deferential toward him, giving him a jewel once in a while, and playing chess with him, one *could* become friends with him. When we reach that stage, we shall have another meeting to decide on the final mission."

The group was silent for a while, weighing Dario's advice. Then they agreed that Dario's plan might work if carried out by someone who was brave, intelligent, and motivated enough to outwit Sadoc. And they all looked at Filocolo. Without a moment of hesitation, Filocolo pledged, "I will do it well. I will do it alone. I will do it for her love or die for her freedom." They applauded his commitment and then left him alone with his thoughts.

And Filocolo had a headful of them.

Chapter Thirty-Four

As he walked around the room, thinking, worrying, hoping and despairing, he stopped in front of a mirror and looked at his reflection. He did not like what he saw and was about to move away when the image in the mirror seemed to change, but not much, just enough to make him look like Florio. And Florio spoke to him.

FLORIO: What are you doing to yourself? Going from one dangerous scheme to another, and all for loving a woman more than yourself? If you don't love yourself, you cannot love someone else.

FILOCOLO: And that is the way I do.

FLORIO: You do not. If you loved yourself more, you wouldn't risk your life for her safety.

FILOCOLO: I will not lose my life.

FLORIO: And who assures you of that?

FILOCOLO: The hope and faith I have in the gods who will help me.

FLORIO: The gods help those who help themselves by staying away from deadly risks.

FILOCOLO: What am I supposed to do?

FLORIO: Leave her alone.

FILOCOLO: I cannot.

FLORIO: Yes, you can if you want to.

FILOCOLO: And what will my life be without love?

FLORIO: Love another one. The one your father likes or your mother picks. Make them happy. They love their only son. Stop this nonsense. A short madness is better than a long one.

FILOCOLO: I can't just stop loving. Besides, people will call me a coward for not rescuing her.

FLORIO: And die because people will talk about you?

FILOCOLO: So, I should just leave her and go back home?

FLORIO: If you want to live.

FILOCOLO: And what will my life be worth then?

FLORIO: More than being dead and buried.

FILOCOLO: Who would kill me if I make myself known?

FLORIO: Whoever will strike you without asking who you are first. Like the castellan.

FILOCOLO: It won't happen. I will soften him up with gifts and compliments.

FLORIO: I doubt it. But even if you rescue her, what will you gain?

FILOCOLO: The one I love and who loves me.

FLORIO: Do you really believe she remembers you? Out of sight, out of mind.

FILOCOLO: How could she ever forget me?

FLORIO: For another lover. Do you think the merchants never touched her? Or the admiral?

FILOCOLO: If the admiral loved her, he would keep her for himself. If she was not a virgin, she wouldn't have passed the magic tree test.

FLORIO: Even if she is still a virgin, she is not worth risking death for.

FILOCOLO: She certainly is, or I wouldn't have risked so much already.

FLORIO: You were a fool for taking so many risks; you will be even more foolish now.

FILOCOLO: Foolish, no. In love, yes. I will use every means, every cunning plan, every force I can muster. I will cajole, connive, fight, beg, buy or steal to get her. May the gods forgive me and help me. I am in their hands."

After this conversation with himself, he became more resolute than ever to rescue Biancofiore. The only problem now was how to enter the forbidding fortress known as the Tower of the Arab. He had to find a way without getting killed in the process.

Chapter Thirty-Five

Filocolo's youthful enthusiasm soon clashed with his scouting inexperience and slowed down considerably the execution of their rescue plans. He went around the tower's neighbourhood so many times that he came to know every stone of every house and street in that area. Yet, he could never bring himself up to even approach the meadow around the entrance.

In the meantime, he reminded his group not to mention his name or their mission to anyone, not to treat him like a leader or even a nobleman, not to meet with or talk to any countryman they might recognise in the streets. Ascaleon reminded him to practise on his chess strategies, some of which he had taught him. Filocolo listened to him and went around public gardens and libraries where people played chess, watching the better players, memorising moves and traps, practising on his own and with older players who were more gracious with him. And so, time passed. Actually, three months passed without any progress. It was as if the gods were testing his patience and devotion to Biancofiore.

And his patience failed him one hot day in May when his desire to be near Biancofiore brought him around the tower once again. There he stopped his horse, let go of its reins as well as of his will power, exclaiming, "If I am to die, since I cannot have you, I must embrace the place that holds you."

And with that he let his horse run up to the base of the tower where he dismounted, walked to the tower and embraced it, kissing it several times.

From the gate post, Sadoc the Castellan noticed Filocolo's irrational behaviour and took immediate action. He called his fully armed guards and ran toward Filocolo, shouting, "What are you doing here, you crazy young man? I don't know what god keeps me from killing you right now. What is going on?"

Filocolo was at first bewildered by the castellan's words and the aggressive stances of the men surrounding him with spears and drawn swords. Then somehow his oft-rehearsed plan surged in his mind, as he pleaded, "Oh my lord, forgive me. It was not my intention to offend you. A snake in the grass must have scared my horse and it ran wild while I was admiring your palace. Still if I have done wrong, I place myself into your hands. Do with me as you please."

Sadoc gazed at him for a long time. Something about this young man reminded him of the First Maiden in the tower. That and his humble response softened his anger.

"Young man, mount your horse and follow me."

Filocolo climbed quickly on his steed and followed

meekly behind Sadoc, who was obviously intrigued by this stranger. He wanted to know more about him.

"Tell me, young man: are you a squire from some distant land? And what are you doing around here?"

Glad to see the change in Sadoc's attitude, Filocolo hastened to answer.

"I am a poor valet from abroad travelling to see the world. In Rhodes I heard so many stories about this tower that I had to see it for myself. If anything, the stories do not do justice to its beauty."

By now they were at the huge door of the tower, which opened for them without a sound. They dismounted and sat by a table. Sadoc was still looking intently at Filocolo.

"Young man, your resemblance to a maiden in the tower saved your life today. You should thank the gods who calmed my wrath when I first saw you—something that happens rarely, if ever."

Filocolo thanked the gods and him several times as he looked at his surroundings. A richly decorated chess board hanging on the wall attracted his attention.

"Sir, do you enjoy playing chess?"

"Indeed," replied Sadoc with some smugness. "*Do you* know how to play?"

"I do, but only a bit," confessed Filocolo.

"Then let us play until it's cooler outside and you can return to the city."

"I would like that very much, my lord," answered

Filocolo.

At a signal from Sadoc, the chess board was brought down, the chess pieces were set up, and two stacks of coins were placed on each side. "An incentive to play seriously," explained Sadoc. Filocolo bowed to him as they began to play.

Not long into the game Filocolo realises that he is a better player than Sadoc and that could be a way to initiate his rescue attempt. Soon he can block Sadoc's king with one of his rooks and with his knight, since the king has one of his own pawns to its left.

Sadoc lays siege to Filocolo's king with many checks, but eventually he has only one move left to save his own king: he must move the rook.

It is Filocolo's turn; he can move his second knight to checkmate the king. Instead, he knowingly moves his rook to safeguard his king.

Sadoc begins to laugh, seeing that he can now checkmate Filocolo (instead of the other way around) by moving his piece forward. And he does. Still laughing, Sadoc rakes a stack of coins to his side of the table, admonishing Filocolo.

"Young man, you have a lot to learn about this game."

To which Filocolo replies, "My lord, this is how fools learn."

The second game begins. The amount of coins is doubled on each side. Sadoc makes funny remarks and mocking faces at Filocolo's plays.

Filocolo does not answer, pretending that the coin loss saddens him greatly. Again, when he is about to mate the castellan, without showing that he is aware of it, Filocolo suddenly tables the game.

The castellan, realising that Filocolo would rather lose the game out of courtesy than to win it outright, thinks, *This, is the most noble and courteous young man I have ever met*. So, before the third game begins, he tells Filocolo, "You must play as best as you know how, and must not spare me as you have done up until now."

"My lord, the pupil can hardly play with the master without being defeated. But if you insist, I will play as best as I know how," promises Filocolo. And he does.

Accordingly, the third game begins and goes on for a long time. Eventually Filocolo has the better of it and the castellan knows it. He begins to get angry and to redden in his face, but the more he plays, the worse it goes for him. Filocolo takes his knight with a pawn and checks him with his rook. Sadoc, angered beyond reason by that move, slaps the chess pieces and throws them and the board to the ground. Coins scatter all over the floor. Silence ensues. The guards are shaking with fear.

Filocolo looks at him and says, "My lord, since it is normal for even the wisest men to become angered at this game, I do not judge you less wise for this. But, if you had taken a good look at your game, you would have seen that I was within two moves from being checkmated by you. I think you saw it, but decided to lose the game to be kind toward me. But I will not let you. These coins are all yours." And he picks up the coins and gives them all to Sadoc.

The castellan is impressed. "In my days I have played with many, but until now I never found anyone who could checkmate me or could be as courteous as you."

Filocolo checkmates him again. "Sir, when it comes to courtesy, you have no equal. For today my life was saved by your courtesy."

It is getting dark. Filocolo is anxious to leave. He demurs to the castellan.

"My lord, it is late and I must return to the city. Therefore, if it pleases you, I will take my leave."

"Young man, if it were not dangerous to travel through these places by night, you would dine with me tonight. But I would like you to return tomorrow to eat with me."

Filocolo does not have to hide his pleasure as he replies, "I cannot deny you anything that pleases you. Your command will be fulfilled."

And with that Filocolo climbed upon his horse and departed from Sadoc, returning to the city somewhat happy. The first stage of the rescue plan had been completed successfully. Maybe the next stage would come more quickly.

Chapter Thirty-Six

Dario, Bellisano, and Ascaleon were happy to see Filocolo safely back with them and overjoyed when he told them about his encounter with Sadoc and their incipient friendship. Then Dario summed up the strategy.

"You have crossed the first bridge and more by appealing to Sadoc's vanity and passion for chess. Now you must work on his other weakness: his concupiscence for gold. So bring him some tomorrow night. I will see to its delivery."

As agreed, the following evening Filocolo rode alone to the tower and was received as a guest of honour by the castellan. A sumptuous dinner, followed by performances of musicians and dancers, took up a good part of the eventful meeting.

At the end of the meal, when nothing was left but the serving of the fruit, a person walked up the hall with a large golden fruit cup covered by a thick veil. To Filocolo's great relief, it was Parmenion who could hardly walk any further because of the great weight of the cup.

He placed it in front of Sadoc and said, "Good sir,

that young man whose life you saved yesterday presents this cup to you with fruits that grow in our country. Moreover, let it be known that he and his possessions are at your pleasure."

Sadoc avidly pulled the veil off the cup to bare its precious contents: gold coins of every size. His eyes grew bigger when he lovingly fingered the largest coins. He was obviously exceedingly happy and grateful as he spoke.

"I feel inadequate to express myself in ways befitting such a gift, so I will not do that. But I still feel obligated to the giver much more than I have ever been."

At that Parmenion made a proper bow and left the room. The castellan then dismissed all the attendants and entertainers so the two of them could speak openly to each other.

Sadoc finally asked Filocolo, "What did I ever or could ever do to deserve such a great gift from a young man who surpasses all others for pleasantry and courtesy?"

"I know that you are the kind of person who could do for me more than any other man in the world. But you already spared my life." Filocolo paused as if thinking before he posed a rhetorical question. "Could anyone ask for more?"

Convinced by Filocolo's hesitation that there was more to it, Sadoc pressed him several times to say how he could serve the youth better, each time diverted by Filocolo with evasive answers. The castellan insisted gently but firmly. At last Filocolo gave in and began his confession.

"My old tutor Ascaleon is fond of quoting this Latin proverb: 'Audaces fortuna iuvat timidosque repellit'— Fortune helps those who dare and rejects those who fear. Since he is right most of the time, I'll dare open my heart to you and share my innermost secret. But if I say anything improper, please forgive me and reproach me like a father. I put my life in your hands, once again. It's yours to take or give back as you see fit. So this is what happened.

"I have come from Spain in search of the girl I love more than life. It would take me days to tell you what I have gone through, mentally, emotionally and physically, since she was kidnapped over half a year ago and sold as a slave. With the help of the gods and some friends I have traced her here, in Alexandria, indeed in this tower. Her name is Biancofiore. She is safe under your careful watch, for which I am most grateful. A beauty like hers can attract unwanted attentions in any other place. I know I am young and foolish in saying this, but at this point in my life I will be satisfied if you grant me one of two wishes: let me die by your hands or let me speak to Biancofiore. You asked me what you could do for me, and I dare say this much: don't let the life that I have because of you perish because of you."

And choked by his emotion, unable to speak one more word, Filocolo stood there, looking straight into Sadoc's eyes as if trying to break into his heart.

Sadoc looked back at him for a long time before he spoke, after clearing his throat a few times.

"Your ingenuity, sincerity, and unshakeable devotion have brought me where I thought no one could. I am already old and I've never done anything noteworthy for anyone. Until now. If I serve you and survive, I will earn great merit with the gods. If I die serving you, I will earn a great reputation with people everywhere. But come what may, I will put an end to your troubles." With that he opened his arms.

Filocolo ran into them (without reticence or deceit) to embrace him like a relative.

Sadoc patted him on his shoulders before he added, "You have asked for something that cannot be accomplished with small hardship, therefore listen carefully.

"In a few days we will celebrate the Feast of the Knights by bringing sacrifices to the altars of Mars and flowers to the temple of Venus. And the admiral sends a basket of roses to the most beautiful of his maidens, which this year is Biancofiore. I will put you in the basket that will be hoisted up the tower to her room. Of course, you will be completely covered with flowers. If you are discovered, as you could be, our lives will be over. If we succeed, you can be with her for several days. If the admiral decides to go up there to eat, as he does at times, I will take you out disguised as one of my sergeants. There is no other way. He has the keys to all the doors, except for this one" —and he points to an open door— "which I am charged to guard. Do you think she is worth my life and yours?"

Filocolo did not hesitate. "Yes, yes, yes. My life for sure. Gladly. I am ready to meet any danger. Yours? I cannot speak for you. But to achieve great things, all great heroes faced great dangers. This is your time to be great, Sadoc. Your time to be a hero." And he hugged him again.

The second stage of the rescue mission had been successfully completed.

Chapter Thirty-Seven

On the night before the Knights' Feast, Filocolo eagerly returned to Sadoc's tower and slept there to be certain that nobody would see him enter it in daytime. But he did not sleep well or much. He fretted about what could go wrong with the plan and he asked every god he knew to help him succeed, but especially Mars and Venus, promising them to burn many cups of incense around their altars.

Early on the next day, Sadoc came to take him where the baskets were gathered and placed him in one of the largest ones. After Filocolo crouched himself in the smallest foetal position he could assume, Sadoc covered him with flowers and roses, reminding him, "Not a sound, not a movement, not a word before you are in Biancofiore's room or we are both dead."

After that he brought it along with the other baskets before the admiral, placing it directly in front of the admiral's chair.

When the admiral ordered Sadoc to bring him the most beautiful basket, Sadoc presented the one containing Filocolo. Thinking of Biancofiore, the admiral took a rose out of it, pulling a wisp of Filocolo's blond hair, but he did not see it. He then ordered Sadoc and others to bring that basket to the foot of the tower and present it to Biancofiore "with love from him".

From there, Sadoc summoned Gloritia, still in the service of Biancofiore, warning her that the basket was being pulled up to her window. While the basket was being hoisted, Sadoc shouted to Gloritia, "Make sure Biancofiore receives this basket before anyone else's."

Filocolo, who did not hear who was being called, assumed that he would be received by Biancofiore. So, when he was delivered before Gloritia, assuming that she was Biancofiore, he uncovered his face. Gloritia, not expecting him, gave out a loud scream. When she recognized him, she reassured him by saying, "Do not worry. I know you," and she covered his face again.

But it was too late. The women around her asked her why she had screamed.

"A bird flew out of the basket and almost into my face. Everything is fine, now."

When she was alone, Gloritia dragged the basket into Biancofiore's room, locked herself in, pulled Florio out, and embraced him with great joy and emotion. Of course, Florio wanted to see Biancofiore. After all, it had been more than a year since she had been taken away. But Gloritia knew better.

"I know you are anxious, but you must wait a little more. As part of today's tradition, the ladies go from room to room, looking at the flowers received,

177

comparing them, making unabashed remarks about the sender—all in fun, and all together.

"Now if Biancofiore saw you, she would not let go of you or go with them. And that would be very bad, even dangerous, if reported to the admiral. So, I must find the opportune moment when she can be with you without missing out in the girls' festivities.

"This is what we'll do: I will put you in an adjoining room, from which you can see her and her friends. But you must be quiet and stay put until night-time. Then I will take you back here and hide you behind the curtains of her bed, which I will lower, for they are now raised—as you can see.

"After everyone falls asleep, including her, you will come out and gently awaken her. If anything goes wrong, I will be very close to both of you and alert you to any danger."

"I can hardly wait to see and hold her, but I will do as you say," promised Florio.

Gloritia then took him into that room and left him there, but not before she locked the door behind him. She then went to Biancofiore, who, along with the other maidens, was going from room to room, strewing rose petals around, singing, playing instruments, dancing, laughing, and just having a joyous time for the entire day.

For Florio, it felt like the longest day in his life to endure—so close to Biancofiore and unable to touch her or even talk to her.

When the festivities ended late into the night, Gloritia prepared Biancofiore's bed, helped her into it and lowered the curtains around it. Only then she pulled Florio from his hiding place and, without making any noise, guided him behind the bed curtains, which were thick enough so that one could not see through them.

Biancofiore lay in bed, but for some strange reason she was restless and could not fall asleep. So she asked Gloritia to stay with her. Of course, Gloritia obliged her, as she had done every night. This time, however, she asked, "Biancofiore, if God would grant you a wish, would you want Florio to be here right now?"

"I would do anything to have him here. I would live in a prison to be with him. I would give myself up to evil spirits if they could bring him here. I do not know if *he* would do this for me."

"What?" exclaimed Gloritia. "Would you put his life in danger to have him in this place?"

"No, I would kill myself before I'd want that. But... if I had him for a while, I would not care about my death."

"Well then," retorted Gloritia. "You cannot have him. He is not here, nor can he come here." She hesitated for a moment before asking, "Is there anyone else whom you would desire?"

"Gloritia! Don't say such things if you love me. I desire or like no one in the world but him. In fact, I dream and desire him so much that sometimes, including now, I feel like I have him on my side, almost as if he were a ghost. Listen, I know he is looking for me everywhere. Maybe he is in this very city right now."

"I bet," Gloritia said with a sly smile.

Biancofiore rolled her eyes in response to what she thought was unnecessary sarcasm. Gloritia kissed her goodnight before going to the next room where she always slept.

But Biancofiore still could not fall asleep. She kept thinking about Florio, imagining his face—probably changed in the last two years without seeing him—whispering to him as she did most nights.

"O sweet Florio, I wish I could now hold you in my arms. How good it would feel to kiss you a hundred thousand times. I would kiss those eyes that made me fall in love for the first time. I would squeeze your neck with my aching arms all night long. Look at this huge bed. I am so lost in it. You could snuggle next to me with room to spare. Oh, dear Venus, since I cannot have him, send me a sweet dream about him. Let him come to me, I beg of you." She sighed long and oftentimes until she finally fell asleep.

As soon as he was sure that she was asleep, Florio undressed himself quietly and put himself between her outstretched arms, pulling her gently between his arms. He spoke to her gently and kissed her with every word.

"Awake, my life, to find yourself happier than any other woman with the happiest man in the world. Awake as you hold the object of your desire in your arms. Awake and take the gift that the gods have brought you."

Having pulled back the curtains, he looked at her under a brighter light. He uncovered her, gazed at her bosom with amorous eyes, and touched her round breasts, kissing them many times. He ran his hands over her private parts and reached the place that encloses every sweetness. In touching her he experienced enough pleasure to transcend with happiness the realm of the gods. He knew he had to awaken her, lest she'd think it was all a dream. And with words and kisses, he eventually succeeded, but not as he had expected.

Startled by the unaccustomed familiarity with her body, she sat up immediately.

"Oh my god, oh, my soul. Who takes me?" whimpered Biancofiore.

"Florio, the one who loves you more than himself. Don't be afraid. All is well."

Biancofiore was breathing quickly, but somehow she quieted down long enough to catch her breath and ask, "Florio? No. You are something evil. My Florio is in Spain."

"I am here by the gods' will. So relax, my love. I am in your arms, healthy, safe, and happier than I ever was. Rejoice with me."

Biancofiore was not quite reassured. She touched his face, his arms, and his hair. She brought him close to an oil lamp burning on the wall.

"Is it truly you? I have dreamed of this so many times. I can't believe it is all real. And I am going to wake up crying for you again."

"No more tears, Biancofiore. It's time to be happy with me," pleaded Florio.

"Happy? I forgot how. Besides, how can I be happy if you are in mortal danger?

"Let's not think of dangers now. Let us enjoy ourselves. We don't know how much time we have while we are in someone else's domain."

Biancofiore answered him with the most luminous smile that had ever graced her face, followed by the longest and strongest embrace to reassure herself of the reality of Florio. That was followed by many kisses and caresses, each trying to double in number and intensity what had received. After a while, Biancofiore stopped long enough to ask, "What happened to the ring I gave you, as my dearest friend?"

Florio promptly showed it to her. "This is no friendship ring. I did not struggle for so long just to find its giver, but to make her my inseparable spouse. Indeed, before there is anything else between us, I will marry you with this same ring, in the presence of Hymen, Juno, and Venus."

Biancofiore had to admit, "Sometimes I doubted

this moment would ever come. I survived praying for it. Now I am determined to make it happen or to die because of it. So let us go and take our marriage vows before our gods."

Having covered herself with a rich robe, she went before the image of Cupid and crowned it with flowers. Then she lighted shining lamps before it and both of them knelt. Florio spoke first and Biancofiore repeated every one of his words.

"O holy god, lord of our minds, whom we have served faithfully since our childhood, look with merciful eyes upon the present deed. I seek to unite this person to me with indissoluble matrimony, a union that no god may harm, no man may divide, no accident contaminate, but which your mercy may preserve in unity. Just as you have always kept our hearts united with your powers, now preserve our hearts and bodies in one will, in one wish, in one life, and one essence. Be you the witness to our marriage."

At that point, Biancofiore stretched her finger and received the wedding ring. Then she rose and kissed Florio bashfully and he kissed her before the holy image. After that she ran into Gloritia's room to show her the ring and her new husband.

Gloritia pretended to be surprised by the events, although she had been listening to it all from behind her adjoining door. They kept their happy excitement to a low level, afraid that the sound of their laughter and joy might awaken the maidens in the nearby rooms. Then Gloritia left them to their delights and went back to her room, with a huge smile of happiness and complicity on her face.

In the celestial abodes their patron gods—Hymen, Cupid, Venus, and Diana—celebrated the ceremony of their protégés with Olympic festivities that made other gods take envious notice.

In the tower of Sadoc the lovers delighted themselves in amorous conjunctions for most of the night. Then overtaken by sleep, sweetly embraced, they remained in bed long after sunrise.

They did this for three days and three nights, during which they told each other their misadventures and adversities when they were not loving each other in every imaginable way. It all was going so well that they became a little less careful about their behaviour. And one day their luck ran out when the admiral ran into their room.

It was to a certain extent Biancofiore's fault: she was a beauty that nobody could forget. Not even the admiral, who had episodes of acute melancholy, often brought on by his obsession to please his master, the king of Babylon. The admiral had somehow discovered that if he looked at Biancofiore long enough, his melancholy would be dissipated. In fact, he believed that she was endowed with every joy-giving power.

So on the third day after he gave her the best roses,

feeling somewhat depressed, he went up to the tower without any company, as usual. His keys dangling from his diamond-studded belt, he went straight to Biancofiore's room, opened the locked door, and entered into her bedroom. To his devastating surprise, he found Biancofiore and Filocolo fully asleep and completely naked on her bed. His eyes bulging with anger and disgust, he drew his sword out and raised it to slay them.

But Venus was watching over them. She flew between them, pushed them apart—as if they might naturally turn over during their sleep—and received the blow onto her invisible and invulnerable body. The lovers continued to sleep.

The unexpected failure to slaughter them gave the admiral a reason to pause and question himself.

"Why should I get my sacred sword tainted with their vile blood? I have guards who are paid to do just that. I'll make an example out of them. And publicly at that."

He sheathed the sword again without awaking them and descended from the tower. At the ground level he found his sergeants awaiting him.

To them he ordered, "Go to Biancofiore's room, break down the door, and seize her and the young man lying naked with her. Tie them both naked and lower them over the main window onto the meadow. Pay no attention to their crying or screaming. Leave them bound by ropes, but not touching the ground for all to see them suffer in shame and pain."

The sergeants followed his order with sadistic joy and pleasure. They indulged in touching Biancofiore while tying her still asleep. By the time she woke up, she was being mishandled and vilified like the worst street whore would be by a drunken mob.

Filocolo suffered the same treatment, but his screaming rage roused Gloritia and every maiden who lived up there. When they asked the sergeants for explanations, they received one answer: "Orders from the admiral. Their vile deed earned them a vile death."

The tower maidens began to pray to the gods for them and lament their own fate, but when looking at Filocolo, they minimised Biancofiore's guilt, secretly whispering they wished they had been in her place then, though not now.

The sergeants hurried to carry out the order of their master as they lowered the lovers perilously down the tower, suspended in full view of the citizens quickly gathering around the meadow. The admiral pondered about their punishment, but not for long: death by fire.

Upon his command the fires were lighted; the two lovers lowered to the ground, still naked, forced to walk toward the burning fires.

Ircuscomos and Flagrareo led a host of archers that would provide security for the execution. These two came from the Libyan nations, their faces bronzed in the sun, their countenance bellicose, their fame as tough warriors.

Filocolo tried to plead for a last favour. "We have lived with and loved each other since childhood. Our bodies were separated, but not our hearts and souls. Let us die with the same flame consuming us, mixing our ashes, and freeing our souls to go away together."

Ircuscomos, never inclined to be merciful at home or in battle, pretended not to hear Filocolo's words. But Flagrareo interceded.

"How can it harm us to grant him one last favour? The flame is strong enough to burn two as well as one. Let him die with her since he sinned with her."

Ircuscomos reminded him, "We are soldiers. We obey rules. We do not make them. Act like a soldier."

Flagrareo obeyed in silence. He tied Biancofiore and Filocolo to separate stakes, yet very close to each other.

The lovers looked at each other with pity and sadness for the other's fate. They talked softly, trying to comfort one another, each taking the blame for the other's predicament.

Then Filocolo remembered his mother's last present, the ring he still had on his finger. He stretched his hand far enough to touch Biancofiore's palm.

"My mother gave me this ring before I left. It has the power to save the wearer from flames and waters. It helped me the night I almost drowned near Naples. Take it; I can pass it on to you. You deserve saving, and by staying alive you will make me very happy in death."

Biancofiore refused to take the ring.

"Your life is dear to others and to me more than mine. Keep the ring and hold my hand. It might help us survive. But let us not despair now. Let's pray to the gods to pull us out of this horrible test."

As the flames approached them, they touched their hands and invoked their gods.

Venus was the first one to hear their prayers. She looked down and saw the fire. Although the ring was helping them, the lovers were still in danger. The archers were poised to strike. Venus went immediately to Jupiter and the other gods, especially Mars, to ask for their help and blessing. With their approval she flew down to Alexandria in a very white cloud and came to the lovers' stakes. With one hand she removed the acrid fumes from the lovers and pushed them onto the soldiers and spectators, creating a very dark and hot cloud that prevented anyone from seeing where Filocolo and Biancofiore were. Onto them she breathed clear and pure air as she revealed herself.

"My dear subjects, be reassured your prayers have touched the heavens. This will be the last peril you will encounter here. Hold on to this olive branch until you are safe. Mars, my forever ally and lover, is bringing your friends here. I will watch over you until they rescue you."

Having said that, she left the olive branch in their hands and disappeared before they could thank her.

The fears of the goddess were justified. Ircuscomos and Flagrareo with iron clubs in their hands were pushing the sergeants to find and burn the youths, but nobody could see them any more or pass through the thick smoke without choking to death.

They resorted to throwing arrows and spears through the smoke, hoping that one of so many darts would kill them. The darts disappeared into the smoke. Nothing reached the victims. No human can fight a god and win.

But humans can fight alongside the gods to help their friends in desperate situations. Such help was about to arrive in the form of the friends who had come to Alexandria with Filocolo.

Chapter Thirty-Eight

After Filocolo had been gone for three days and three nights, Ascaleon, Bellisano, Dario, the duke, and the others were dismayed and fearful by his long absence and lack of news. Ascaleon was particularly worried that something pernicious might have happened to his hot-blooded pupil while dealing with Sadoc and his sergeants.

That night, Ascaleon had a dream in which he saw Filocolo wounded in many ways and asking him for help. When Ascaleon asked him who was attacking him, Filocolo replied, "Two Libyans and their soldiers want to burn us alive by order of the admiral. Aren't you coming to rescue us?"

Even in the dream, the flames were so hot that they awoke Ascaleon. Perplexed by the realistic vision, he dressed himself quickly and called his friends to tell them about the dream. Some believed him; most were not so sure about what to do; all agreed to go out and find out for themselves. The streets were bubbling with people discussing scandalous happenings at the tower. They heard about a naked lady and a stranger being condemned to death. The description of the stranger was close enough to fit Filocolo. They were so stunned by the news that they did not know what to make of it. Did Sadoc betray Filocolo? And why the death sentence for Biancofiore?

It was then that they were approached by a tall, rugged knight with red hair, riding a war horse. He, who looked more like a god than a knight, addressed them with godly authority.

"Good knights, why do you delay? Filocolo is in great danger. Take up arms and follow me quickly."

Hearing Filocolo's name removed any question or hesitation from their minds. They rushed to get their weapons, climbed on their horses, and pushed their way through the crowd. When they arrived at the embattled meadow and saw the thickness of the smoke just below the tower, they began to think that it was too late to save him. But Ascaleon would not stop there.

"I do not know what you want to do," he told the group, "but I will die fighting to avenge my lord's death. If any of you wants to go home, this is the time to do it. Anyone else, follow me."

Their unanimous answer was, "We are all with you in one will."

They struck their horses into a gallop and followed Ascaleon into the dark smoke where the unknown knight had stopped to encourage them forward. And here they found Ircuscomos and Flagrareo inciting the hostile mob to put the two lovers to death.

Ascaleon tried to see Filocolo through the smoke, but to no avail. His companions looked around, saw no sign of him either, and looked back at Ascaleon for orders. They came with sober urgency.

"Since Filocolo is probably lost in those flames, we will avenge his death upon his executioners. And if no one slays us, we will kill ourselves to follow him in death. No one wants to report his death to the king."

Having said that, he urged his horse toward Ircuscomos, aiming a sharp lance into his shield. The lance broke harmlessly into pieces. In response, the Libyan raised himself on the horse to strike Ascaleon on his head. Ascaleon eluded the blow, pierced him with a lance, and pulled him off the horse. Ascaleon then drew his sword and slashed the Libyan's left shoulder so hard that it almost sent him with the shield to the ground. Ircuscomos felt the sharp pain, but still managed to strike Ascaleon on the head harshly enough to stun him. Enraged by the unexpected vigour, Ascaleon went back to the Libyan's wounded arm and cut it off the shoulder. But the Libyan would not admit defeat, even as he received more blows on his shield. Unable to absorb the strikes rained on his shield, he finally dropped it, turned his horse around, and ran toward Alexandria.

The din of the battle increased, as the group followed the courageous example of Ascaleon and fought valiantly against so many enemies. That was true especially in the case of Parmenion who attacked

Flagrareo, unafraid of his fierce appearance and his cohorts, striking him so fast and so often as to leave the Libyan half-dead on the ground.

Bellisano too, already an old knight, but an expert master of arms and combat, was doing wondrous deeds. Following Ascaleon, he killed or wounded as many of the horde that dared to face him. Nobody could resist his smooth and deadly blows.

On the other hand, the duke, fighting a very strong and aggressive Turk named Belial, could not have withstood him if Menedeon had not come from the side with an axe, taken from a warrior he had just killed, with which he struck the Turk on the head and wounded him mortally. At that time, he and many others ran away toward the sea with all their armour and horses and drowned in the rushing waves.

Messaallino and Dario, who had come closer to the smoke than the others by running after two knights, found themselves trapped in the midst of many foot soldiers who had managed to kill their two horses. But even on foot, those two friends managed to kill so many enemies that a large mound of bodies surrounded them while a rain of arrows kept falling on them. The two were using captured shields to protect themselves, but the enemy arrows kept coming and some were piercing their bodies.

All seven companions, weakened by the fighting and the wounds, were dangerously close to the point of exhaustion when the fierce knight with red hair went into action. He gathered them behind him like an ancient Greek phalanx and, with his bellicose appearance and dexterity, instilled so much fear and shock into the hearts of the hordes that every one began to run away from the battle field to avoid the devastation wrought by the re-energised group. With all eight of them striking quickly across the meadow, the battle was soon over.

The wide expanse of the meadow was almost empty now and the noise abated as well. The only people left there, besides the victors, were the wounded and the dead.

From the tower balconies many maidens watched in tears and sighed for the safety of Biancofiore and the horror of the slaughter. Several, horrified by the sight, retired to their rooms. Some, fascinated by the events, would not move. Others offered prayers to the gods for the safety of the small band of victors.

At this time, the victors approached the smoke barrier. Sad for their deathless victory, and wishing death, they did not bandage their wounds, but looked over the field and marvelled at what the few of them had accomplished. Each one thanked the great knight, not realising that he was a god, and asked him how he came to be so strong, brave, and victorious. The knight smiled, but answered no question.

The group now wondered how to end their lives.

"Let us jump into the fire now," suggested Dario.

"No," replied Ascaleon." Let us give them first a burial, so no one else would contaminate their ashes."

"But how do we find them?" asked Dario. "We still can't see beyond the smoke."

On the other side of the smoke, Filocolo heard the voices, but did not recognise them because they were covered by the wailing of the wounded and the thickness of the smoke. Yet he knew that those people would help, so he shouted as loudly as he could.

"Any knight who is out there, please listen to me. By the grace of the gods we are still alive inside this dark cloud. Cross over to where we are and untie our bindings."

When his familiar voice reached the ears of Ascaleon and the others, he rejoiced immensely, but, as wise as his age had made him cautious, he wanted to be sure, so he asked aloud, "Dear son, we thought you were dead, and maybe you are and some evil spirit is trying to dissuade us from joining you. If you are alive, we want you safe on our side. If dead, we will soon be on your side."

Then it was Biancofiore who, recognising the voice of Ascaleon, cried out to him.

"Oh dear, dear teacher, believe what you hear. Your Florio and I are alive, unscathed within the burning flames. I burn more to see you than do the woods lighted for our immolation. Let me wait no longer to hug you."

But try as one might, no person was able to go

through the wall of smoke surrounding the two lovers. Their friends talked to them while waiting for something to happen or someone special to come and break down the impassable barrier that had saved the lives of Florio and Biancofiore.

Chapter Thirty-Nine

On the other side of town, a different group gathered to report and understand the highly unusual events of the day. Ircuscomos, with his arm cut off but otherwise alive, and other wounded or stunned soldiers went to see the admiral straight from the battlefield.

"Lord, see how some unexpected foes have wronged us," muttered the Libyan with a bow.

"Who are they? How many of them? What do they want?" asked a very angry admiral.

"Lord, I don't think there were more than seven or eight fighting against our whole group, doing with their weapons some incredible things. I don't know who they are, but I am sure they wanted to save the young man and girl whom I believe to be dead."

"What do you mean, *believe*? Didn't you see them die? Didn't you light the fire?" the admiral's voice raised with his anger.

"Certainly," replied Ircuscomos. "But as soon as the fire started, the smoke turned against us instead of rising to the sky and enveloped the prisoners like a very strong wall, impenetrable to sight, people, and spears. While we kept shooting arrows at the prisoners, a band of fighters attacked us under the leadership of an enormous warrior whose appearance frightened whoever tried to face him. All total, nothing is left on the meadows but dozens of dead and wounded fighters. And I still do not know what happened to the condemned ones."

The anger of the admiral reached unsustainable levels. His face was livid, then red, then burning with fury. He would personally go after those attackers. He ordered every man to be combat-ready and to follow him immediately. They did, out of fear and curiosity mixed with hope for revenge, encouraging each other with shouts and other noises made with drums, trumpets, and horns to signify battle. But as soon as they reached the road around the meadow, all the horses stopped, rose on their hind legs in fear, turned around, no matter how harshly they were whipped, and ran back to the city with or without rider. Moreover, the hair of every man curled up on his head and fear paralysed their every move. No one had the courage to cross into the meadow. No one, but the admiral who could not believe in such endemic cowardice of his men. So he tried to go it alone.

The result was the same. He became more frightened than the others, turned around the reins of his running horse, but he himself did not know why. He tried different manoeuvres to distract the horse and himself. Nothing worked. And suddenly the thought occurred to him that he had done it all wrong.

"I was wrong in condemning two youths to death without any deliberation. What do I know of who they might be? Why would the gods do those things for them? Because it had to be the gods' doing when six or eight men defeat a whole company of soldiers. And what about the impenetrable cloud? And the horses afraid to cross this road as they have done so many times before? And this dread in my heart? What am I afraid of? I need to make peace with them. I need to save the youths if they are still alive. I need to make amends. That's what I need to do."

After such thoughts, he decided to take action. He disarmed himself, put on a white robe, had an olive branch brought to him, climbed on a fresh horse draped also in white, and tried to cross the road. Unlike the times before, nothing stopped him and no dread pounded in his heart. He proceeded toward the knights, still led by the frightening knight mentioned by Ircuscomos, and addressed them in a humble and trembling voice.

"With the symbol of peace in my hands, I ask you for a truce. In revenge for the villainous death of two youths, against whom I was unreasonably cruel, you killed many of my knights. This meadow green in the morning is now red with their blood. If the youths' death has not been amended by our losses, let my humility compensate for what's missing. When begged, the gods often forgive men. Through their example, forgive me."

Ascaleon looked sternly at the admiral, yet he spoke like a benevolent teacher.

"Actually, a person who refuses peace to make war where peace could exist deserves the anger of the gods. We fought to die and avenge those youths, but the gods have saved them and us from death. Like us, they are alive and well.

"And you should rejoice, realising that the gods' wrath, provoked by your injustice, has fallen not on you, but on your people. Let that lesson be your punishment for trying to kill friends of the gods.

"The past cannot be changed, but you can make amends for it. If you seek real peace, we give it to you. Now go and release those whom you have bound and treat them fairly, lest you provoke the gods' anger and ours."

The admiral agreed immediately to the terms and swore by his gods to preserve the peace. He then ordered his people to drop their weapons at once and use every means at their disposal to break through the smoke barrier and free the innocent youths.

There was no more need for that. The rugged knight who had helped them in battle ran with his horse into the smoke and disappeared behind it. Immediately the smoke rose to the sky in the form of a reddish cloud that flew away into the heavens. The fierce, red-haired knight was nowhere to be found.

But no one noticed it, busy as they were untying Florio and Biancofiore and covering them with elegant garments. Ascaleon, the duke, Parmenion and the others dismounted from their weak horses and embraced the lovers, weeping from joy and relief for their safety, asking if they were hurt in any way. However, they were still vigilant to make sure that no harm would come from the crowd of apparent well-wishers and new admirers. And the admirers came from everywhere.

From the windows and balconies of the tower, one hundred maidens cheered Biancofiore's rescue and threw roses at her. What had been a funereal morning now became a mid-day celebration of life, and an afternoon of improvised mirth.

The astute admiral became part of the festivity when he ordered fresh horses for the rescuers and the two youths and made them his guests. "If it pleases you, let us go to the city to fully celebrate the good fortune granted this day by our gods."

And so, they rode toward the city, with the streets lined with curious citizens discussing the extraordinary events they had witnessed and commenting on the beauty and nobility of the two youths. Biancofiore was surrounded by her rescuers while Florio rode alongside the admiral, who kept looking at Florio as if he resembled someone he knew, but could not recollect. In fact, he was so full of curiosity that at last he had to ask.

"Young man, if you find it in your heart to forgive

my intemperance as I have forgiven yours by making peace with your group, would you please tell me who you are, from where you came, and how you were not even singed in the fire?"

Florio looked at him steadily to gauge the depth of his sincerity before he answered. "Dear sir, since I have accomplished my mission, I can now reveal my identity. I am Florio, the only son of King Felix of Spain." Then pointing to his hand, he added, "This ring from my mother, who came from these parts, saved us from the flames."

At the sight of the ring, the admiral began to shake, his lips quivering. "Forgive me, Florio, but now I am even more curious. You claim to have an Egyptian mother. Are you trying to be a congenial peacemaker or are you telling the truth? I needed to know that because—" The admiral stopped there unable to continue.

"I would not lie to you about my parents, and I would not disavow them. I am their son. That cannot be changed," assured Florio with some testiness. "Why do you even doubt it?"

"Because the only person who had such a magic ring was my sister Kandia. If that is your mother's name, you found your love and your uncle in Egypt." And he stretched his arms out to embrace Florio even as they were on their horses.

Florio returned the embrace with amused surprise.

"It certainly is, dear lost uncle."

"Oh, happy gods and people. I, the brother of your mother, almost killed you today. I will never be happy anytime I recall this incident. To amend my rashness and ignorance, from now on dispose of me and my kingdom according to your pleasure."

It was just as joyous for Florio to be recognised as a relative as it was for the admiral. And he told him so. "Sir, for what happened today you are not to be blamed. I alone, rash beyond propriety, dishonoured your house after enduring so many hardships to reach it."

"Things attained through hardship are appreciated more than those freely given to us," the admiral advised him in a smiling avuncular tone.

To him, Florio responded obligingly. "A wise observation, Uncle. But let us put all that in the past, forget about it, or pretend that it never occurred. Then the only thing left for us is to enjoy this moment."

The admiral, pleased beyond reason with the nobility and goodwill of his new relative, passed on the prodigal news and his euphoria to everyone around. By the time they reached the city, they had become the happiest entourage to travel the roads of Alexandria since its most famous resident's return from Rome seven centuries earlier.

They moved slowly through the elegant streets of the city and eventually reached the royal court, where they dismounted their horses and were greeted by joyous attendants who ushered them into the great hall. But when they entered it, they were met by the trembling and double chained Sadoc and Gloritia. By order of the admiral they had been seized to find out how Filocolo had gone up to Biancofiore. If found guilty, they would be executed.

The scene moved Florio to near tears, but he did not cry out. In fact, he pretended not to know them as he winked at them to be silent. He then pleaded with the admiral.

"The gods would be pleased if on this day of jubilation, we forgive anyone for mistakes made without malice. Enough people have died unnecessarily. Let us not add these two to the pyres."

Anxious to show the sincerity of his peace promises, the admiral ordered them to be untied and to join the festivities without any fear. The joy in Florio's heart rose to his face and did not escape the appreciative looks of his two accomplices.

The feast began as soon as the royal staff medicated the wounded companions with precious ointments, dressed the two lovers in royal vestments, and prepared exotic dishes of food and desserts, accompanied by the finest wines from Greece and Italy. The conversations flowed with the wines until late that night. The guests were then given the best rooms in the palace for a much-needed and welcome rest. Eventually Florio and Biancofiore fell asleep too.

Chapter Forty

On the following day, Florio asked the admiral if he could make some religious sacrifices.

"Before anything else, I want to fulfil the vows I made to our gods. They have kept their promises; I want to thank them by keeping mine."

Pleased to oblige his nephew in as many ways as he could, the admiral made all the proper arrangements, which included the procurement of animals, fruits, wines, spices and other gifts.

Florio then visited all the temples throughout Alexandria, decorating each of them with myrtle crowns. In the process he sacrificed a bull for Juno, a cow for Minerva, and a calf for Mercury. He offered olives to Pallas, fruits and cereals to Ceres, wines to Bacchus, combat armour to Mars. To Venus and Cupid and to every celestial, marine, terrestrial, and infernal god he offered precious gifts and perfumed fires on their altars. This time he did not forget Diana.

Biancofiore, Ascaleon and his companions, along with the admiral and prominent citizens, did the same, absolving the numerous pledges made to diverse gods for each other's safety.

Having fulfilled the vows made on the night of their happy conjunction, Florio and Biancofiore returned to the royal house accompanied by many residents who still talked about their beauty and their near-death escape from the flames. They all pointed to the sky, giving credit to the gods for the fortuitous outcome. Then it was time for another banquet with the admiral and his retinue. And it was at the end of this banquet that the admiral asked Florio, "Tell me, dear nephew, is it your intention to make Biancofiore your true spouse?"

Taken aback by the question, Florio felt a surge of anger that could have easily put an end to the festivities, but a stern look from Ascaleon reminded him to act with civility and respect. And he did.

"I have never wished anyone else as my wife but Biancofiore. Even before the gods granted her to me, there was no room in my heart for any other woman."

The admiral must have expected that answer because he had a prompt response.

"Then, it is not proper that such a high union has been made so furtively. Therefore, after I divulge your noble origin to my subjects—who wonder why I honour you as I do—you will marry her in their presence with a ceremony and a feast befitting such a marriage."

The applause that followed told every person present that such a proposal was very pleasant to Florio and his group. And Florio spoke for them.

"Dear uncle and gracious host, we are pleased and

honoured by your idea. So much so that any arrangement you make will be most warmly accepted by us."

With that the preparations began. First of all, heralds were sent to all corners of the city to announce the forthcoming royal wedding. Then the bodies of the dead were buried properly. Court doctors medicated the wounded. The royal treasurer comforted their families with discreet compensation and, in some cases, lifetime sinecures. The battleground's meadow was cleaned and re-sodded to erase any disturbing reminder of the recent battle. The meadow around the Arab's Tower was the place where commoners came to see spectacles in which the pursuits of life or death were exalted by the rulers of Alexandria. It was the best venue for the ceremony envisioned by the admiral.

On the day charted by the royal astrologers to be the most propitious for the wedding, the admiral returned to the meadow, now completely landscaped with fresh-cut flowers and bushes. Dressed in royal vestments shining with gold, he descended into the great court along with Florio and Biancofiore, accompanied by many noblemen and by singers, dancers, and musicians to entertain the people already gathered on the meadow.

In a slow and deliberate procession, they walked up to a platform from which they could be seen by all and were seated on silken pillows—the admiral between

Biancofiore and Florio.

After receiving a loud ovation from his subjects, the admiral rose to his feet and signalled with his hand that he wanted to speak. When the crowd and the celebrants were silent, he began. "Gentle men and women, citizens of all ranks and races, I present to you Biancofiore, a noble descendant of Scipio the African, and Florio, son of my sister and King Felix of Spain. I have been told that these two have loved each other since childhood. Separated by fate and force, they came here where they almost met their death for the same reasons. With the gods' help, they survived and now wish to solidify their love through matrimonial bindings and our blessing. I have therefore decreed that you witness this wedding, enjoy the feast afterwards, and honour them according to their high rank."

He turned toward the tower's windows, which were crowded with maidens gaping enviously at the wedding party.

"I extend the invitation to all the ladies in the tower as well. They will be most welcome to our banquet."

The admiral had barely finished his speech when the trumpets sounded to signal applause. It came as traditionally expected but, this time, also by popular choice. When the clamour simmered down into near silence, priests dressed in ceremonial robes walked solemnly to the platform, carrying images of their gods, which they displayed to the royal party and the people.

They hung wreaths over those images while piously invoking Hymen, Juno, and other gods to grant the couple a gracious beginning, a solid middle, and a serene end to their marriage, while keeping them conjoined in peace and unity. Then the chief priest slipped the wedding ring on Biancofiore's finger— albeit for the second time—while the couple promised each other life-long faithfulness and love. At that point the priests, the newlyweds, and the crowd began singing hymns of joy and love accompanied by many instruments. The wedding ceremony was over. The festivities were just beginning.

First came the warmest congratulations of their companions. But who could better congratulate Biancofiore than her tower roommates? For the first time they were allowed to come out and mingle with the wedding guests, hugging and kissing each other with love and happiness and a sense of short-lived freedom. Their arrival brought the feast to a higher level of merrymaking, with songs and dances that endeared them to the crowd. Their entertainment was followed by the arrival of exquisite foods prepared by the royal chefs and distributed freely to all comers. Games were ordered and groups participated in them under different flags to indicate their neighbourhoods or countries. The changed winds of Fortune had turned everything around. People who were fighting each other only days before now drank and danced together. Maidens who had cried over Biancofiore's death now rejoiced in her wedding. Fires lit for the lovers' execution were now stoked for cooking savoury meats.

As Ascaleon wisely observed, "Only people who have problems should cry over them. I see no such people here."

The feast lasted for seven days, during which gifts were given to the newlyweds, and promises made and kept by several people.

Mindful of the "Peacock Pledges" made to Biancofiore on King Felix's birthday, Duke Ferramonte served as Biancofiore's cupbearer throughout the celebrations.

Parmenion came to the bridle of Biancofiore's horse and led it all the way to the royal palace every night.

Menedon jousted with many young nobles of the city, completing intricate horse manoeuvres and javelin throwing that greatly impressed the populace.

Ascaleon would have kept his pledge too were it not for all the wounds he had sustained that prevented him from doing so. Besides, Biancofiore insisted on his remaining by her side.

Messaalino, away from his territories, was unable to fulfil his pledge to give her ten date plants with gold-laden roots. Along with Ascaleon, he vowed to keep his promise upon their return to Marmorina.

Unfortunately, they had to wait ten months for the

weather to be fair enough to set sail for the homeland. When it was, Florio expressed his desire to leave to the admiral.

"You have been more than an uncle to me since we met. If it were not for my filial duty to see my aging parents and my subjects to reassure them of my safety, I would stay forever with you to whom, after the gods, I owe my life, my wife's and my group's welfare. As it is, I also worry that the families of my companions who probably grieve for their prolonged absence. Therefore, I beg you to let me leave with your blessing."

"Then," said the admiral, "I will definitely encourage you to leave. It is only right that your family enjoy your presence more than anyone else. I will have your ship fully ready to sail when the winds are propitious with the gods' will."

Chapter Forty-One

Within days, the ship—loaded with generous gifts and supplies—was boarded by the anxious passengers, not without emotional farewells from their new friends and relatives and proper sacrifices to the gods of the sea and the wind. To be sure, the admiral ordered three other ships to escort them over open waters. The ships pushed off out of Alexandria's port by the efforts of strong rowers before they could raise the sails to the winds for a smooth and fast passage to Rhodes, Bellisano's residence.

Here, at the insistence of Bellisano, Florio and Biancofiore disembarked to meet his friends and family, who were extremely relieved to see them safe and healthy. They stayed there for only two days, during which they were treated like heroes returning from great victories, before they resumed their voyage. Bellisano wanted to accompany Florio to Marmorina, but was persuaded by him to stay home since his aging body needed more rest than hardship.

While the winds were blowing nicely in the right direction, Florio wanted to fulfil his promise to Sisife, to stop over in western Trinacria, so named for the three promontories that give Sicily its triangular shape. Of course, Sisife was excited to see them together and asked them for all the details of their adventure. They stayed up most of the night to tell her and her family their love story while savouring local delicacies enhanced by the sweetness of their Marsala wine.

On the following morning, the sailors came to take that happy lot back to the ship headed for Napoli, the place where the siren Parthenope died when unable to seduce Ulysses with her song. The wind picked up while they were still in view of the Aetna volcano, but under the able steering of the captain, three days later they reached the Neapolitan shores and landed into its calm port. No sirens were sighted or heard along the way. At that point Florio decided to complete the remaining trip by land, much to the relief of everyone aboard. Upon unloading the ample supplies and treasures given to him by the admiral, Florio kept some men with him and sent the others back on the ship to travel to Marmorina with news of their imminent return to his parents, relatives and friends.

After so many days at sea, even with propitious winds, Florio, Biancofiore and his retinue felt the need and had the opportunity to relax and enjoy the scenery and the comforts of Napoli. So they toured the places most visited by people or mentioned by historians. On one day they sought the warm baths of Baia, and Sybil's Cave, through which Aeneas was allowed to enter the world of the spirits. Next, they sought the ruins of Cuma, and its nearby sea whose shores abound with green myrtle, and ancient Pozzuoli with its surrounding antiquities, alternating a soaking in mineral waters with a dip in salty waters or a fishing trip. Sometimes they let their falcons give chase to smaller birds, or their hunting dogs rouse rabbits and boars. Most evenings they spent enjoying music and dances with old and new friends.

Chapter Forty-Two

And so it happened that one day, Florio, Biancofiore, and a group of noble men and ladies entered a little forest while chasing a deer that had sprung out of a bush at their arrival. As soon as Florio saw it, he took a spear from one of his companions and threw it forcefully, hoping to hit the deer. But the spear missed the animal and hit a tall pine, cutting off a piece of hard bark that fell to the ground. Suddenly blood issued from the bark and with it a doleful voice.

"Oh, miserable fates. I did not deserve the pain I bear, and you, still unsatisfied, continue to stab me. I envy those who are allowed to die when they wish it." The voice stopped there.

Stunned by the arcane voice, Florio and his friends stood there, looking at each other and at the bleeding pine, unsure as to what to do or say. Eventually Florio took a deep breath and responded in a plaintive voice.

"Forgive us, most holy tree, if any deity hides in you. I hurt you by accident, and I am ready to make any amends that will cleanse your injury and pacify your wrath."

The trunk breathed heavily through the bleeding

wound as if trying to inhale its pain before it spoke again.

"Young people, no deity is enclosed within me, but I forgive you anyway. Your regret is enough and acceptable. Besides, while I cannot harm anyone, men and beasts sometimes harm me."

"Then pray tell us who you are and why you have been relegated here," inquired Florio, "so we may honour your memory among all people."

To which Biancofiore added, "By coming to know the truth about you, we can retell it to those who do not know, and they, in turn, moved by pity will pray to the gods to lessen your pain and enhance your fame."

"Your courtesy and sweetness make me eager to please you. My father was a shepherd called Eucomos, whose steps I followed through my entire childhood. When he was still young, he built himself a bagpipe that, when finished, was the best-sounding instrument in the meadows. Eucomos played it so often and so well while tending his sheep that eventually it attracted the attention of many fair ladies who asked him to play for them. He did. They liked it and returned to hear him time and again.

"The most beautiful of them was Gannai. Fond of his music more than any other, she urged him to play for her alone. Her beauty reached the heart and mind of Eucomos, who wished he could possess her. Cupid, instigator of vagabond minds, descended from

Parnassus and added hope and desire to the poison of his arrow destined for the hapless Eucomos. The burning flames of love stimulated him enough to seduce Gannai through his music. And so one day he convinced her to come into a recessed green meadow where the sheep could graze and rest while he played for her. His music changed to sweet words to reveal his love for her through many flattering promises. Among them, he vowed to be like her father had been to her mother, and to only play for her at her request. She believed him naively and consented to his pleasures from which she engendered two sons: I was one of the them. She named me Idalogo.

"But a short time later she abandoned us for reasons unknown to me. Eucomos returned to his fields with us two. There he met and married another woman and fathered other children. Since the two of them had no more time for me, I left his house and came to this forest to ply the only trade I knew: shepherding.

"It was here that I befriended Calmeta, an extraordinary shepherd from whom I learned the science of astronomy. As I lingered in these fields, I came to know many visitors who came to inquire what the stars had in store for them. Some were beautiful ladies, but one above all attracted me. She could see my interest in her. She could feel my desires. She knew that I loved her immediately and acted accordingly. She seduced me. Soon after we became lovers, which I thought we would be forever, she tired of me and left me for a younger man. I was absolutely destroyed by her behaviour—which reminded me of my mother's. I roamed the fields and the forest, crying over her cold-heartedness, but I did not leave this place. I could not because it was the only place where I felt safe and at home.

"So I began wishing death to alleviate my pain. But since my appointed time was yet too far away, Venus felt mercy for me and decided to stop my pain altogether. First, she changed my feet into roots, then my body into trunk and my arms into branches. Finally, she turned my hair into leaves before girthing me completely with hard bark. My human semblance was gone and so was my inner pain. Until today.

"As you can understand, I have little faith in worldly things and especially in women, in whom no good, no stability, no trust, and no reasoning can be found.

"For that reason, if I could, I would inveigh against the gods, reproaching them for giving to man—noble above all creatures—a companion so contrary to his virtue."

The wretched man had barely finished his story when Biancofiore rose to her feet to be closer to the broken bark and responded in a resentful tone that surprised the group.

"Idalogo, Idalogo, why blame all the good and

faithful women because an evil one betrayed you and hurt you?"

"If I thought that what happened to me was the exception, I would not feel so strongly about it," replied Idalogo. "From the beginning, the world was and still is filled with their betrayals. But since you rose to defend the good ones, won't you tell me why and who you are?"

Biancofiore was quick to answer.

"I arose to defend the virtue that each one should first practise and then defend because I am free of the sin of which you accuse every woman. I am Biancofiore who has had bad luck since birth, yet loved only one man, and is now happy."

"What? Are you the same Biancofiore known through the world for being faithful to her Florio even in the face of death? If you are the one, you have reason to be hurt by my words."

"I am that one," answered Biancofiore.

"Then you deserve singular praise and many apologies. I should have excluded you when I spoke ill of all women. Your deserved fame is more of a wonder than to hear and see me in this form. So, what happened to Florio?"

"My Florio has spoken with you. He is here now. How could I be happy if I were without him?"

"Blessed be the gods. If they are on your side now after so many misfortunes, maybe there is hope that I too could reach a similar outcome."

Florio came closer to the trunk as he spoke. "May Fortune hear your pleas, Idalogo. But I simply wonder how you came to hear our love story since it is hardly known within our country."

"How your exploits were known in these parts I could not tell you," replied Idalogo. "But I can tell you how I heard them. As you see, my leaves offer welcome shade in summer, and the ground around me is soft with grass and flowers. People love to come here and talk about themselves, about others, about events that have impressed or horrified people. So I heard your story, which I judged no lesser than mine, feeling that I was not alone in the hardships of love."

It was getting dark as the sun was falling behind Mount Abetino. Florio thought it was time to go home. So he took leave from Idalogo.

"May the gods grant your wishes as you granted ours to hear about your troubles. But before we go, is there anything we can do to please you?"

The trunk seemed to shiver with delight as Idalogo answered.

"Since you asked, yes. You can do much. A young man aware of my troubles recently told me that the lady I loved had been turned by the gods into white marble next to a small fountain in the caves of Mount Caperrino, just past the dark grotto. I was sad to hear that, but still uncertain about her identity. If you could go by there, would you offer to her some comforting words for me? Oh, and do not leave before you put back in its place that hard bark slashed by your spear. With that I bid you adieu with the grace of the gods."

"I shall do both," promised Florio as he placed the bark in place.

The tree took it back as quickly as iron sticks to lodestone.

They left the mysterious place wondering about Idalogo's story and his uncanny metamorphosis. But wise Ascaleon reminded them of a Latin dictum: "*Quisque faber suae fortunae est.*" [Each is the blacksmith of his own luck.] But sometimes one needs the gods to light the fire in his forge."

The group was silent for the rest of the trip home.

Chapter Forty-Three

They left early, the following day, before the Neapolitan sun became too hot for the horses. They were not sure where the grotto was, but it had to be around the Falerno vineyards whose owners used such caves to store their powerful wines. After roaming around the hills for quite some time, they heard the voices of people shouting and laughing. They moved toward that site, hoping to find someone who could guide them.

In a clearing they saw many shepherds watching muttons ram their heads into each other, encouraged in that sport by their owners. The visitors were welcomed to enjoy the spectacle.

"The winners of the contest will be auctioned off to sire many healthy sheep," explained an old shepherd.

When asked about the location of the grotto with a marble fountain, the old man pointed to a hill nearby. He could not leave the herd to guide them there, but two of his daughters could. In fact, they did so very graciously. They had been there before several times to gather fresh water in their home barrels.

Florio and his company reached the grotto after a short walk and came to a wall of bushes that kept the fountain out of sight, even as one could hear its gurgling run. A white life-sized marble block overlooked part of the water. In front of the marble was a beautiful pomegranate tree with thorny rose bushes on both sides.

Florio refreshed his hands and face with the cool, clear water, then seated himself next to the white marble, as to be heard by all and began to say, "I am from a land west of here, but I have heard of a hard-hearted woman, as hard as this marble, who caused somebody so much pain and sadness as to desire his death if he could not have her. Have you heard any such story before?"

Alcimenal, one of the two sisters, replied, "Those of us who live here have heard it before. Our ancestors told us that in their time, only the water and the grotto were here. The grassy knolls, the ample trees' shade, and the fresh clean water brought visitors from Napoli every day to escape the heat of their city. So it happened that one day during summer, four beautiful ladies did just that and lingered under these trees, while enjoying sweets and drinks.

"It was mostly the gift of Bacchus that loosened the tongues of those ladies, who in a short time began to disparage the supreme gods while praising themselves and their lasciviousness as more deserving than the gods. The one named Alleiram (*Mariella*) sat down by the white marble; the second named, Airam (*Maria*), sat by the pomegranate; and the third, Annavoi (*Iovanna*, placed herself to the left and to the right of Mariella, each holding hands with Maria.

"Mariella, the more talkative of the four, spoke first. 'When I was young and naïve, I was told that Diana came here to bathe herself, and the Nymphs, Naiads, and Dryads came here to rest and to hide. How stupid of me to believe that. People dedicate places to gods and goddesses and believe them to be holy. They have gods in their midst, but they seek them in the stars. Women can make men do anything they want. So why revere Venus, Cupid or Diana more than women? Remember Helen of Troy? She started a war that the gods could not stop. Can Jupiter's lightning or thunder be feared more than our wrath? Mars is nothing compared to what we can do. Would this place be revered if not because of us? The fact is that when it comes to power, I am greater than Venus. And I'll tell you how I know.

"'To begin with, my bloodline needs no introduction, unlike that of those who call themselves gods. The same goes for wealth; Juno, goddess of riches, envies me. I have a huge number of relatives. Do I need to say that I am very beautiful? That anyone who passes by my gorgeous house stops to look at me? There is more. Although everyone likes me, I do not like everyone, even if I pretend to. I am good at giving and receiving compliments, which I'll swear to be truthful, but they are not. Cupid has tried, but failed to hurt me with his darts. My lovers have literally fallen all over themselves and into my wiles. I laugh at them and take up only with those I believe will please me.

"'One of those, a good-looking and well-spoken young man, caught my fancy. I played with him, enjoyed him, and finally gave him what I pretended to deny him all along. But after a while, I tired of him and watched his happiness turn into tears. He begged me to return to him and prayed Venus to melt my heart. She came to me in dreams and visions. I ignored her. In short, the young man remained a loser, wasted himself away, and eventually turned into a pine.

"'I never went back there. If I did, I would cut the tree down with an axe and burn its branches into ashes. So where is Venus' power? I did it all. I should be honoured as a goddess.'

"'And so you should,' replied Agnesa. 'We are neglected for no reason. Do we deserve it? Look at Luna, the Moon Goddess. She changes her face every month.

"'She hides during the day, and comes out at night when so many bad animals roam and do mischief to humans. And Diana? She turned Actaeon into a deer, which her dogs devoured, just because he had seen her naked. She is so unfeminine she must be a hunter because she can't be a lover. And Venus? If she is so beautiful as the poets say, why did she let handsome Adonis (who was so crazy about her) get killed by a boar? Look: I do not hide my beauty to men. I do not change my face with the seasons. I do not eclipse. I stay beautiful. I am loved and worshipped by many men who will do anything for me no matter how difficult or costly it might be. I should be called a goddess by all rights.'

"'By all rights and by all people,' chimed in Maria. 'Those gods are frauds. They claim to see the future and to know the past. But it is not true. If they did and had all the power to punish sinners and criminals, why do they let the outrages that we see every day go unpunished? If they have such superior nature, why would they mix with us imperfect mortals? Why are they deceived by the tricks of simple maidens or change their shapes to deceive those maidens? If they are strong, why change into a bull to deceive Europa? If beautiful, why change into golden rain to deceive Dannae? If wise, why make hurtful promises to Semele? If we do not rate above them, we can at least consider ourselves their peers without any trouble from them. Right?'

The foolish companions laughed their approval before the fourth one, Iovanna, concluded. 'Why do we even talk about them? They have no power, no wisdom, no beauty, and no pity. They are merciless tyrants and usurpers of someone else's attributes. What have I not done already to spite Diana, the so-called vindictive goddess? With my beauty and my voice, which could make me a siren, I took away from her five hunters of various ages and turned them into blithering lovers whose hearts I ripped and threw away. For that I suffered no vengeance from Diana. Why? Because the power of the injured party was not there, and vengeance always strikes the less powerful. I saw none of it.

"'So I do not believe in gods and goddesses any more. We are goddesses, and those men whom we like are our fellow gods. I ask you: what celestial kingdom could be more pleasurable than this one, our own? We are beautiful, smart, and powerful and will rule men as long as the world will last. Therefore, we alone deserve the honours that Jupiter and other gods have unjustly enjoyed.'

"The four women laughed and mocked the gods for a long time, and time after time.

"But the gods were not amused by those irreverent musings. No less inflamed than when they were attacked by the beastly daring giants, they stirred with sudden anger within their celestial seats, which produced a frightening sound as if all thunders and lightnings occurred at the same time. The world was covered with running dark clouds, moved by tumultuous winds, which shook the earth and the seas. They were ready to scourge the planet with their furor, but Venus, Phoebus, Luna (Moon), and Diana prevailed upon them to let them take matters in their own hands. These gods entered the grotto and found the women still blaspheming them without fear of divine judgement.

"Venus turned first to Mariella. 'You wicked woman, you brag about the delayed vengeance and threaten to do worse? It is here now and worse for you. You, spurner of love, will receive none. You will no longer please anyone, see anyone, be loved or pursued by anyone. You had no compassion for anyone; no one will pity you. The tears of the one who was once yours will cease. He will enjoy a sweeter woman than you were. Hard and immovable to my wishes, you will change into hard marble, with no trace of your beauty, in this grotto.'

"As Venus spoke the transformation began apace. Mariella wanted to ask for mercy, but the oncoming cold, which had already frozen her tongue, did not allow it. The icy hardness moved rapidly from her head down fusing her face, arms, and legs into one shapeless trunk that was soon white, hard marble.

"Phoebus appeared then in front of Maria and spoke with a sweet, sarcastic voice. 'Well, young lady, you boast of having deceived me by hiding your heart from me and depriving me of dear gifts? Now I will return the favour. You will change into a tree immediately. But since you had the audacity to demand to be equal to or above us, you will have your branches distorted downward so that even a very small man will pick your fruit from the ground.

"'Oh, but there is more. Since you were a concealer of your heart to everyone, your fruits will open up to everyone. And since you exalted the radiance of your beauty, the juice of your rind will be used to dye anything darker.'

"Within a very short time, her wretched body was reduced into this pomegranate.

"Agnesa, between those two, did not try to escape or ask for mercy. That did not pacify Luna, the Moon goddess, who approached her sternly. 'So, you besmirch my beauty for no reason? I never offended you, unless you count the times when I shone my light on your furtive love-makings while you were trying to escape me. You claim that I change so much every month, but I am beautiful only once. Fine: you will become a small shrub, whose pretty flowers will bloom once a year, for a very short time, fall to the ground, and turn into the colour of my eclipse.'

"Immediately Agnesa's fair body changed into a fragile plant, her legs became hairy roots, her arms thorny branches, her dress green leaves, her face a plain white rose.

"Lastly came Diana, who confronted the suddenly-shy Iovanna with unabated anger. 'Delayed vengeance does not amount to diminished pain. As an abuser of my subjects, your new appearance will always evoke the evil deed committed. You will become a fragile plant bearing only one vermillion flower. You will have five green leaves signifying the ages of those you alienated from me—two adults, one young man, and two adolescents. Its yellow centre will represent the gold you took from them.'

"As she spoke, Iovanna began to change into the form assigned to her by Diana.

"This done, the gods returned to their kingdoms. The wind removed the ominous clouds. The earth resumed its placid course, and the sky regained its clarity.

"The gods' just revenge had restored balance and tranquillity into the cosmos."

Florio thanked the young ladies profusely for guiding and enlightening him and his retinue. But before they left, he turned to the fountain to keep a promise made to another human plant.

"Oh sacred fountain, by that pity which moved them to just wrath, I pray you, if in some way you can intercede for Idalogo, to do so. Let your sweetness soften the hardness of the pretty stone loved by him until the last pain."

At these words, the inside of the marble appeared to tremble, but the gentle hardness of the white surface, holding perhaps her face, did not let it be revealed. With that, Florio exited the grotto and returned to the city with his people.

Chapter Forty-Four

Just before they reached the city gates, he recognised his old friend Caleon from afar and called him to join them. Caleon did so gladly, but Florio noticed that he was not the happy person he once was. Upon discreet inquiry, Caleon admitted that Fiammetta, the queen of his life and of Napoli's social life, had left him. He was heartbroken and unable to find his way out of that painful rejection.

Florio, who had known similar dark days without Biancofiore, urged Caleon to come with him to Marmorina. The voyage and the company might distract him out of that depression and maybe open his heart to some new love. Caleon took his advice to heart and accepted the invitation. He was warmly welcomed by all of Florio's company.

It was time to leave Napoli and travel north toward Marmorina. They moved as slowly or as fast as the tortuous trails allowed them through the towns of Capua, Caserta, Frosinone and Latina. It was here that Florio remembered Fileno, whom he had last seen and spoken to in the guise of a fountain upon a wooded hillock named Certaldo. Anxious to meet him again,

Florio took his retinue to that meadow covered with green grass and sat there with them to take a respite from the late afternoon sun.

As the sun came down, Florio took Biancofiore by the hand and guided her toward that fountain. And there he spoke to her with some trepidation in his voice.

"Dear love of my short life, will you tell me the truth about a matter still close to my heart?"

"Of course, I will," said Biancofiore. "Why would you even ask? I've never lied to you."

"Just so. Do you remember Fileno to whom you gave your veil out of love? Did you ever miss him after he left town to escape my anger?"

Biancofiore's cheeks turned embarrassingly red, as she answered him.

"I thought of him many times because of the letter you wrote to me accusing me of deceiving you. I gave him the veil out of duty to your mother, not out of love. I wish the gods could erase such memories from my mind."

"Would you like to see him?" Florio then asked her with an impish smile.

"Yes, I would," Biancofiore replied without hesitation. "But only because I pity his parents who are grieving over their son just like yours do. You left yours because of me; he left his because of your unprovoked wrath."

"You are right to scold me for that. But young

lovers fear and hate every rival. Still, you shall soon see him. Not as a man, but as the fountain he was turned into out of grief for loving you."

Biancofiore, Gloritia, Ascaleon, the duke, Menedon and all the companions lit a ceremonial fire on the meadow so the gods would bless their good intentions. They sat down upon the grass and looked at the fountain bubbling through the two springs in its middle, as it was wont to do in the past.

Biancofiore, who had never seen it before, marvelled at the behaviour of the waters and was about to comment on it, but Menedon spoke first to Florio.

"Gracious lord, I hope not to displease you when I say that Fileno was very dear to me. Since your wishes were granted, you must not be fond of someone else's ills. I feel great compassion for Fileno and pray to the gods to remove him from his misery and return him to his human shape."

"May the gods turn against me if I do not wish for Fileno's return to a life among us," reassured Florio. But there was no conviction in his voice.

As they were speaking, the bubbling turned into a gurgling voice that soon became clear and audible to all.

"I seem to recognise your voice, and I do feel your compassion. May the gods hear your wish and save you from a similar fate. But in spite of all, I lack only one thing to live happily even in this state."

Biancofiore and even those who had heard the

voice before were astounded by the humanity of the speaker. Menedon asked the question for everyone else.

"Tell us what it is. Maybe we can pray to the gods that it be granted to you."

"I only wish to regain the good will of my lord Florio, who was once your companion," replied the fountain. "I lost it because I loved his woman purely, albeit unknowingly. I did not commit any sacrilege, betrayal, or rebellion for which I would surely deserve this and more. Even so, if Jupiter and the gods forgive their offenders when they repent, why not me? The grace of forgiveness is the greatest victory over evil. Therefore, pray for my lord's grace toward me."

Menedon and the others turned to Florio for his approval. It came quickly and sincerely.

"Young man hiding your form within these waves, take comfort. The grace of your lord is given back to you. Therefore, present yourself as you were before him."

The gurgling of the fountain gave way to a happy voice.

"Immortal gods, to whom nothing is impossible, use your great power to return me to my original form before my lord and friends."

A thunder was heard, though no clouds could be seen, and the thunder became the sound of rain gushing through rocks and trees, and then the bystanders saw the waters coagulate in the middle, abandon their grassy bed and erect themselves in a human form, with the head, arms, body and legs quickly becoming solid, living tissue in its finest details. Soon the naked handsome figure of Fileno emerged as if from a cool shower in the hot Neapolitan summer.

Biancofiore and Gloritia demurely turned around and looked away from the scene. The men pulled Fileno out of the hollowed place and walked him slowly, as one who had been dormant for a long time, until they came before Florio. Florio motioned to him to come forward. Fileno almost stumbled to the ground as he knelt before him and asked for his forgiveness and good will.

Florio raised him with his hands and embraced him to reassure him of all that. He then ordered that Fileno be quickly dressed in elegant clothes, his hair and beard shorn and his face made tidy.

Fileno was then presented to Biancofiore, who smiled at him with tears in her eyes. He bowed to her slowly and deeply, and in a way that could not be regarded but lovingly. A keen observer, like Ascaleon, would have noticed, from the way Fileno looked at Biancofiore, that the old flame was still burning in his heart, not doused by seasons of flowing water.

But at that moment only joy and gratitude and a sense of accomplishment pervaded the visitors as they returned toward the city. It was nearly dark when they reached it. As the events of the past days were recalled, the thoughts of the weary travellers flew across the mountains to their homesteads in Montorio and Marmorina, still a month away by plodding horses and mules. Roma was only six days away.

Chapter Forty-Five

Gloritia, who knew the area from the days as governess in Lellio and Julia's house, could practically smell the sweet air of the Eternal City in which she was born. Her homesickness, kindled by the burning desire to see it again, pushed her one day to broach the subject as she and Biancofiore were looking at the green scenery from their high balcony.

"My dear young lady, do you see those rolling hills leading to the distant mountains? Behind them is Roma, where your parents lived and, I am sure, their relatives still do. I promise they would welcome you like a queen. Don't you want to meet them?"

"I think so." She hesitated. "And I have wanted to see Roma since we read Ovid's poems with Master Ascaleon. But I wouldn't want to delay Florio's return to his parents."

"The delay would be short. It's only a few days' ride from here. You'll never be this close to famous places visited by pilgrims from every country on earth."

"I can only do what pleases my Florio. Besides being my husband, he is my lord for many reasons. Wasn't I raised and nourished in his house? Wasn't I sought by him through many nations? Wasn't I delivered by him from death? Twice! If I ask him, he would not deny me anything. But what if something happens to his parents while we are vacationing in Roma?"

"Well then, why don't we go without him. He can always send a messenger to bring us back."

"After being separated for so long, he could never be without me for even two days. He is constantly afraid that the fates will strike me again. And me in Roma? My relatives would snatch me away and marry me to someone else."

"Your parents' families would never do a thing like that. They are noble people."

"So were Florio's parents until we fell in love. No, it behoves him to see his aging parents first. After that I will ask him to visit Roma and my relatives. We have endured so much. We can endure this short term. Until then, hold your desire patiently."

Gloritia realised she could not win her over. "I will wait for as long as it pleases you," she replied as she left Biancofiore alone. But to herself she prayed, "Dear God, let it happen soon."

Chapter Forty-Six

God must have heard her prayer.

That very night Biancofiore had a wondrous dream. She seemed to be in a place unknown to her, somewhere above a large and beautiful city built upon seven hills and crossed by a languid river. Levitating in the sky above the city was a goddess-like lady so beautiful that Biancofiore wished Florio would never meet her. Her garments were made of silk and gold that matched the colour and sheen of her hair. The lady smiled at her, her teeth gleaming like stars, as she descended through the air toward the awe-struck Biancofiore. There was something familiar about that lady, although Biancofiore had never seen her before, and that something made Biancofiore want to touch her, but she could not. Close, but out of reach, the lady looked at her as if waiting for an introduction. Biancofiore's curiosity finally prompted her to speak.

"Oh, beautiful lady, with the face of a goddess, I was praised often for my looks, but if my Florio would see you, he would easily cast me into oblivion in spite of all his love for me. I would be honoured to know who you are so that I may describe your beauty to my friends and family."

Without moving her lips, but still smiling radiantly, the lady answered her.

"Oh, dear daughter, my beauty has made many people happy, but has also caused great harm. You are eager to know me, yet this past day you refused to come and see me and know me. I am your mother and your city. For you I have lost your father and mother. For you two Roman families have been waiting in despair. Therefore, come to see me without delay. Your maker wants it; I want it; you want it. Your destiny awaits you. Fulfil it."

Having said that, she disappeared into the brightness of the sky into which she ascended.

Biancofiore was so stupefied by that dream that she slept no more that night. As soon as Florio awoke that morning, she told him what Gloritia had suggested and what the lady in her dream had said. And she concluded, "I will understand if you do not grant my wish, but if it is possible without upsetting your plans, we should visit Roma now, while we are young and so close to this famed city. Maybe the dream is a portal to places of my past and people of our future. And maybe it is just a dream. Shouldn't we find out?"

She looked at him, her eyes wide open with expectation mixed with imploration.

It was a look that Florio could not resist, let alone ignore.

"Dear spouse, whatever pleases you is a joy for me. As soon as you are ready, we will leave."

"My lord, timing is at your bidding. But if my desire were to be followed, we would be on the Via Appia as soon as possible."

"And so we shall," promised Florio.

He saw to it that all the mules, horses, and carriages were loaded for the trip by the following morning. When they were all set, he forbade all to reveal to anyone who they were without his permission. Then dressed as pilgrims, they mounted their horses and rode toward Roma.

Chapter Forty-Seven

The pilgrim Florio and his followers reached Roma within a week. They entered it quietly, two dozen among hundreds who came daily to visit or to trade in the capital of the western world. They took residence in a large hostelry, near the ancient palace of Nero, and began visiting the most famous places and wonders that had survived attacks by the Vandals and revolts by the volatile Roman citizenry. No one paid more attention to them than they would to any everyday tourist freely circulating around the arches, forums, boulevards, and holy and unholy places that filled the city. No one, that is, until the day Mennilio Africano, brother of the slain Lellio, recognised Ascaleon even under his pilgrim clothes and called out to him.

"Hey, holy Ascaleon, does your sanctity deprive us of your words because we are sinners? Why do you pass by without talking to us?"

Being called by name, Ascaleon turned around and recognised Mennilio.

"Not at all, dear friend. The complete opposite made me fear to speak to you."

They embraced many times and rejoiced together,

reminiscing about the old times and their friendship with Lellio. Then Ascaleon introduced him to his companions.

"These young friends of mine came here to see for themselves the wonders of Roma, which I described to them many times. We have already stayed here several days, and are just making our last tour around."

Mennilio would have none of that.

"You have offended me by staying in a hostelry instead of my house. I have not seen you since my brother left us. Did you forget how much I loved you? Why, we were as close to each other as we were to Lellio. You and your companions *must* stay with me while you are in Roma."

"But we have so many people here," protested Ascaleon, looking for a way out without insulting the hospitality offered. "We have women here. Wives and maids."

Mennilio offered a quick and practical solution.

"Your women will stay with our women, and your men will lodge with our men."

Realising that Ascaleon was being forced into an untenable position by not giving away their identity, Florio covertly consented to what Mennilio wanted, much to Ascaleon's relief. Thus, they entered the great palace that once belonged to Lellio and Julia. Biancofiore did not have any idea where she was. But Gloritia did. She had lived in that palace most of her life.

Without any hesitation, Ascaleon forbade Gloritia to reveal to Biancofiore the identity of their hosts. He was obeyed, of course. But then, it was Florio who wanted to know who and what their hosts were. And he asked Ascaleon, of course.

"What? You don't know where you are and in whose house?" Ascaleon pretended to be shocked.

"Of course, I do," said Florio. "I am in Roma, in Mennilio's house. But who is he? If I knew, I wouldn't be asking you."

Ascaleon sat down facing Florio, like a teacher to a pupil, to discuss some grave matter. "Your hosts, Mennilio and Quintilio, are the brothers of Lellio, Biancofiore's father killed by your father. Lady Clelia, who honours Biancofiore so much, is the sister of Julia, Biancofiore's mother. This is the house where Biancofiore was conceived. Now do you see where Fortune has landed us three years after we left Marmorina in search of our Biancofiore?"

Florio was silent for some time, but only long enough to absorb the impact of the revelation. When he spoke again, he did so in a subdued and rueful way.

"Fortune is still toying with us. She put us in the house of my father's victims. Now I have serious reasons to fear recognition; Romans are notorious for never letting offences go unrevenged. So how do I get out of this predicament without a massacre?"

Ascaleon shook his head, pondering on the gravity

of the situation before he answered.

"You and your young companions have roamed the world without being recognised. This is no different. Nobody knows you here. If you want to leave, we can do it tomorrow. But if you want to make peace with your new relatives, we first must know their hearts. So, this is what I suggest: keep quiet until I learn how they feel about you."

As always Ascaleon was wise and right. And almost as always, Florio heeded his advice.

Chapter Forty-Eight

While they waited to discern their best course of action, Florio and Menedon set out one day from their lodgings to admire the beauties of Rome, which they found to be as numerous as they were astounding in so many ways and places. As they walked, they came upon a beautiful temple with the name Saint John Lateran inscribed on its front side. They entered it and on the fore wall they saw the painting of a man dying on a cross with perforated hands, feet, and ribs. As they looked at it, puzzled by the gruesome portrayal, an older gentleman came toward them and spoke to Florio.

"Young man, you stare at the effigy of the Creator of all things as if you had never seen him before."

To him Florio responded gracefully. "Without any doubt, friend. I have never seen him before."

"And how can it be," said the man, "that you have never seen this if you are one of the followers of his law?"

"Truly, I know neither him nor his law," Florio informed him.

"Then what law do you follow? Whom do you worship?"

"I follow the law of my country and of my people. We worship Jupiter and his immortal gods to whom— as many times as we need them—we light fires upon their altars and offer incense to receive the things we need."

"Then you are an idol worshipper, a pagan," shouted the man.

"If you say so," replied Florio, surprised by his tone.

"Then why do you live among us, the people of God? Don't you know that as you used to set traps for us, we now do the same to you? Since you do not follow our law, do not contaminate this sacred temple. Get out of here." The older man was increasingly upset by Florio's answers.

"How can I follow a law I have never heard of before? You look like a learned person. Instead of being angry at me, why don't you tell me about your gods. I am always willing to learn something new."

Softened by the sincerity of Florio's words, the man responded in kind.

"It's a long story. It needs time to tell. Patience to listen. And humility to follow. I fear it might be tedious for a young man to hear."

"If the telling isn't hard for you, listening won't be hard for me," replied Florio.

They sat on a prayer bench and talked and listened for a long time. Ilario, the teacher-priest, told Florio and

247

Menedon the story of the creation of the world by God and all the events narrated in a book called *The Bible* until the crucifixion and resurrection of his son, Jesus, about seven centuries earlier.

At the end of the narration, Ilario concluded, "Our God gave himself for our salvation. Now who does that? A servant chooses death for the freedom of his master, a father for his son, a sister for another, but here you have a lord choosing a vile and prolonged death for us, servants of sin. We are so perfectly loved by Him that He left the beauty and comfort of His kingdom to become flesh and die for our redemption. Would any of your gods do that?"

Florio had no answer for him. He remembered what his gods had done for him, but he chose not to mention it to Ilario for fear of revealing himself and thus endangering every person in his retinue. Besides, he was a Roman priest in Roma. Could he be trusted? If that Judas disciple had betrayed his God-man, couldn't his priest do just as much? And what kind of God hangs from a cross? Didn't he have the power to save himself, or at least to make himself invisible?

That day Florio left Ilario with many questions and doubts in his mind. He needed to talk to someone. Biancofiore? No. She could not understand his state of mind. Besides, she saw him as a mentor, a leader. She would be so confused by his confusion. He needed a more mature mind. An informed yet independent mind. Ascaleon's.

So, that evening, after ordering Menedon not to reveal what had transpired that afternoon, he took Ascaleon into his room and told him everything.

Chapter Forty-Nine

Ascaleon listened patiently to Florio's recounting of his conversation with the learned Ilario. When he had finished the story, Ascaleon put an arm around his shoulders and walked him toward the window. He pointed to a palace on the Palatine hill.

"That's where I lived for ten years before I joined your father's court. And while I was here, I learned about Christianity and other religions. I rejected none. I favoured some. I learned from all. As a future king, you should too."

"Does learning a new law demand rejecting the old? Must I renege the gods I worshipped all my life? And order my people to renounce them?"

"Would they listen to you? They might obey you, but will not abandon their ancestral gods. Not quickly and never completely."

"Do we have the power to cast away gods as if they were used garments?"

"I hear thundering in the distance. Jupiter is getting impatient with us."

"Shouldn't we fear the wrath of the gods if we turn our backs to them?"

"The question is: were the gods created by men or by themselves?"

"The gods are immortal. Men cannot destroy them. So what should I do?"

"Adapt. Be a Roman in Roma; a Spaniard in Spain. Look around you. New churches are built over old Roman temples. Pagan festivals have become Holy Feasts. Days, months, and planets are still named after our gods. The moon and the sun still share the same sky and lighten the same earth. Day and night follow each other. Old and new follow the same cycle. Adapt to survive and thrive."

"So the new days are a reinvention of the old days?"

"Look. Have you forgotten my history lessons? The Olympians who replaced the Titans were replaced by Roman deities. Christianity was born from Judaism. Islam just branched off Christianity. Religions are like fashions. Clothes, colours, designs vary, but they still serve the same purpose: to make people look and feel good even in the worst days of the year. Religion does the same by promising eternal happiness to the believers. But if it is forced on people, they will resent it.

"As a king, never give your people cause for grievance. Give them bread when they're hungry, wine when they're sad or glad, blankets when they're cold. People with full stomachs do not rebel. They will thank your God—or theirs—for you."

"Good advice from my royal counsellor. I will need it when I sit on that throne."

"It is really Juvenal's *Panem et Circenses* formula. But etch it in your heart for I will not be around to remind you of it."

Florio turned quickly toward him, as if an arrow had struck his back.

"What? You'd leave me when I need you the most? And for what?"

"To go home."

"Home, as in Montorio or Marmorina?"

"No, home, as with my ancestors."

Florio understood, but could not admit it. "You look as healthy as ever. Your mind is clear. Your gait unfaltering over the thousand steps of Roma's stairs. Why do you speak of leaving?"

"Because I hear the last grains of sand falling down my life's hourglass. And there is no way to inverse it. Nor would I want to. My work is done. Yours is just beginning." He started to walk toward the door, then stopped to give Florio hearty advice. "Send Fileno home. Today, if possible. He's still in love."

"But I forgave him. I gave him back my trust."

"The heart obeys no law; follows no rule. You should know that."

Florio stood there, transfixed by the double burden of Ascaleon's revelation.

"Are the gods already punishing me for doubting them?"

"Why blame them if you don't believe in them?"

"I don't know what to believe any more," cried Florio. But he knew what he had to do.

Chapter Fifty

That same evening, he called the entire retinue to his chamber. With Biancofiore by his side looking at him to discern the reason for the meeting, he spoke to them in a most serious tone.

"Over the past three years we have survived many harrowing experiences together. We have become a real family. And it is as a member of this family that I speak to you now.

"Lately I have been talking to Ilario, a priest of the Roman Empire's religion, which has shrines even in Spain. He told me the story of his religion from the creation to the crucifixion of the son of God, whom they call Jesus Christ.

"From my part I told him about my father's attack on the Roman pilgrims travelling to Compostela's shrine just before my birth, and our odyssey after Biancofiore's abduction and rescue that brought us here.

"He assured me that although I can't be blamed for my father's actions, the victims' family is still seething with revenge. They do not know my identity, but that could change at any moment.

"Ilario will not expose us, but to avoid new

bloodshed, he will try to reconcile our families, provided I embrace his religion.

"I am intrigued by the prospect, but I will not make a final decision without your advice. There is no doubt in my mind that the safety of this group depends upon my acceptance of the new God and the rejection of our old gods—something not to be taken lightly for whatever I do will affect everyone here.

"I have sought Ascaleon's counsel on that matter, and I will follow it.

"Since our ways are bound to be challenged by the Roman emperor, a strong supporter of that faith, I will send Fileno to announce our homecoming along with Ilario's priests who will preach their religion to anyone who wants to listen—without coercion, without ridicule, and without persecution.

"My father might oppose them, but in my reign, everyone will be able to practise their faith as long as it doesn't impinge on other people's. That's all I have to say. What are your thoughts on this?"

The group was quick to voice their concerns. They spoke at once among themselves and to Florio. No one could understand anyone until Ascaleon restored silence with the calming gesture of his hands. But they still had questions to ask.

The first question came, understandably, from Fileno.

"I will do as you command, my lord. But wouldn't

I be of better use to you here, fighting by your side if it came to that? An older companion might be better suited as a news herald."

Florio, who had expected the question, answered promptly.

"The dangers down the road will test your mettle just as much. Take some companions with you and leave as soon as you can. Our families have been waiting for us long enough."

Fileno bowed to him and left immediately, but not before one last long look at Biancofiore.

Gloritia, Biancofiore's motherly attendant, spoke next.

"What you have told us is very serious and frightful at the same time. I was raised here as a Christian, as was Biancofiore's mother. Your conversion, if it happens, will bring us closer to each other. But" —and she looked knowingly to him— "don't you have something else to reveal to us? Especially to Biancofiore?"

Biancofiore looked at her and at Florio with puzzlement. Did they know something she didn't?

Florio nodded gravely. "I know what you are referring to, and I thank you for respecting my wish to be silent on the matter." Then turning to Biancofiore, he said, "This was your parents' abode. This is the place where you were conceived."

Biancofiore took a deep breath to inhale the weight of the revelation and another to be able to speak.

"I am home," she was able to utter before she began to cry. "For the first time in my life I belong somewhere." She looked around as if she had just entered the palace. "My mother lived here. And my father too." She turned to Gloritia. "You often told me of my relatives in Roma. Who are they?"

Gloritia was quick to answer her.

"Lady Clelia is your mother's sister, and lords Mennilio and Quintilio are your father's brothers." She pointed to an alcove by the fireplace. "And in that alcove, there was a statue of Saint John whom your mother invoked to have you. *Benvenuta a casa tua!* [Welcome to your house], Biancofiore. You belong here."

"I can't wait to embrace them. Can we send for them at once?" pleaded Biancofiore.

"Not yet," replied Ascaleon. "I haven't told them who you really are."

"But we will as soon as they assure Ilario of our safety," informed Florio. "Which, he said, they might do quickly on my official conversion," he added ruefully. "But you still haven't told me how *you* feel about it."

This time Biancofiore did not hesitate.

"My husband and my lord, I must confess that Gloritia has been teaching me the Christian way for some time now. I need no prodding to embrace my parents' faith. In the words of Mary: *Ecce ancilla domini. Fiat mihi secundum verbum tuum.*"

Ascaleon smiled approvingly as he translated to the group. "Behold the handmaid of the lord. Let it be done with me according to your word."

Florio hugged her as he spoke tenderly to her. "And I will do no less for you, my queen. Your religion will be my law."

Those last words were heard by Fileno eavesdropping behind the door. With a glint of lust on his face and a surge of revenge in his heart, he left the palace—hatching a plan to finally possess Biancofiore. And maybe even the king's crown. He whipped his horse into a gallop as a handful of companions followed him, looking at each other, wondering what had happened to their usually level-headed friend. It would take at least two weeks to reach Marmorina... if the horses did not collapse under them. They knew nothing of the tempest churning inside him, stirred by a passion denied for over three years.

Chapter Fifty-One

Ilario did not delay in filling his promise. On the following noon he sent for Quintilio, Mennilio, and their women to come together to their church. When they were seated, first the men and then the women, all eager to hear the reason for such a meeting in the middle of an ordinary day, Ilario spoke to them.

"A wondrous thing has reached my ears today. A young man and his friend approached me in this place and asked me about its origin and meaning. He knew nothing of our religion so I told him about it to fulfil his heart's interest. When questioned about his origins, he said he was from Spain. When asked if he had ever heard of a valorous Roman pilgrim named Lellio, he informed me that Lellio had been slain by the king, who mistook him for an enemy invader. Julia, his wife, survived long enough to give birth to a beautiful girl who was raised by the queen of Spain, along with a son she bore on the same day. The children, growing and studying together, fell in love and eventually married, against his old father's wishes. So when the young man becomes king, Julia's daughter will be a queen. Imagine what that will do for your noble house and for the Holy

Roman Empire to have a Roman queen on whom we could depend to defend our western provinces from the invading Moors. The future king of Spain wishes to meet you in peace, but he is afraid, and rightly so, that you might want to revenge upon him your brother's death for which he bears no blame. In my opinion he should be forgiven in peace. Pope Gregory would be extremely pleased to see this turn of events as you would to see your niece as a queen."

The assembled relatives remained speechless for a while, looking at each other for advice or opinions. None came as they showed no great sadness for the long-past deaths or joy for the present discovery of a living niece. Finally, Quintilio spoke for the group.

"For as harsh and bitter as it was to lose our brother, that much sweeter and dearer it will be to find our niece. As to how to put that offence into oblivion, we will follow your advice, knowing that you would not propose anything to tarnish our honour."

"And I won't," assured Ilario, "under any circumstance. Therefore, if he wants your peace, grant it to him. And if he comes here, receive him honourably. When you welcome a niece queen into your house, Roma will welcome Spain back into her Holy Empire."

The family members discussed the proposal briefly yet ardently among them. At last a consensus was reached and announced to Ilario.

"We can promise you on our word of honour as

noble members of the church that we will receive them in peace and with due honour and respect."

"I demand no more of you," said Ilario. "Go and, when I summon you, come to me."

The group returned to their homes while continuously talking about Ilario's revelations.

Ilario went immediately to see his superiors, who informed the Pope of the reconciliation plan and the benefits thereof.

The Pope gave his blessing to the plan, leaving its implementation to Ilario.

Chapter Fifty-Two

Biancofiore—left alone with Gloritia in the palace of her father—was pining to finally be recognised by the aunt and her family as their niece. Within her she burned to tell how she was honoured by her mother's sister and her father's brothers, and likewise to make herself known to Clelia.

Gloritia had a somewhat similar but agonising feeling about the recognition. Clelia, to whom she had been a close friend as a young child, now burdened with many years, did not recognise her and neither did one of her brothers she had spotted as a regular visitor of Menilio.

As she and Biancofiore talked about the burden of having to pretend ignorance (by Florio's request), Clelia came in and, being joyously received by them, interrupted their conversation to narrate what had transpired at the church.

Florio broke into their conversation to give a sombre sign to Biancofiore—who already seemed to instinctively recognise Clelia as her aunt—so they would not be discovered then and there.

Biancofiore closed her eyes and bit her lips to hold

back her spontaneous desire to embrace her aunt. Her head, this time, prevailed over the urgings of her heart.

At that very moment, a servant came to the room to tell Florio that a fellow pilgrim wanted to speak to him about their plans for future visits to nearby shrines.

Florio, who had no such plans, understood the gist of the message and left the room with the messenger. As he had presumed, the pilgrim was Ilario, waiting downstairs in a room near the stables.

Ilario informed him of what was to happen.

"Your wife's relatives have promised to meet you in peace, but, since I told them you are coming from Spain in a few days, you will need to follow this protocol.

"Take Biancofiore and your companions to a secluded place outside Roma, where I have made arrangements for your stay. When I send for you, dress like the son of a king that you are and come into the city to meet Biancofiore's relatives. With everyone's cooperation—and God's help—it will all come to a happy fruition."

Florio thanked him vigorously and promised to follow his plan to the letter. And he did. The retinue took their leave from Quintilio, Mennilio, Clelia and Tiberina ostensibly to continue their pilgrimage. They were told to come back at any time for a longer stay. Florio promised they would as soon as possible.

Florio's retinue travelled to nearby Albalonga to a

large country inn where they kept to themselves most of the time or walked through the wooded hills while waiting for Ilario's message.

Ilario was a busy intermediary. Not only did he keep in touch with Mennilio and Quintilio about the presumed travels of the king's son, he also sought the help of Pope Gregory—informing him of the arrival of the young prince, convincing him with subtle prodding to meet the youth with a solemn procession at the gates of Roma.

Only when all the preparations were completed did Ilario announce Florio's arrival to Mennilio and Quintilio, urging them to come out of the city and receive him graciously and honourably—as they had promised. And they did.

Chapter Fifty-Three

The beautiful culmination day wished for by Biancofiore, prayed for by Gloritia, and nervously awaited by Florio finally came. Early in the morning everyone in the retinue had forsaken the pilgrim clothes and camouflages and donned magnificent vests, dresses, and armaments that shone in the sun and revealed the rank and beauty of the wearers.

Florio rode a well-groomed horse ahead of his companions and squires. Biancofiore followed, dressed in green velvet decorated with gold and precious stones, her blonde hair set in a high coiffure by skilful hands, her head covered by a thin veil upon which was pinned a crown beautiful for its craftsmanship and jewellery.

Ascaleon and the duke, albeit at a slow pace, escorted Gloritia and many ladies-in-attendance who had accompanied them from Alexandria. They were all wearing splendid dresses and robes.

From the gates of Roma came a procession of noble men and women, headed by Ilario, Quintilio, Clelia and Tiberina, to meet the foreign guests. When they were close enough, they dismounted from their decorated horses and bowed reverently to Ilario, who introduced

Florio to them.

"Noblemen, here is the son of Felix, king of Spain and husband of your niece. Honour him and receive him in peace as you have promised and you should."

Florio quickly dismounted from his horse—along with his retinue—bowed respectfully to them, and walked toward Ilario who introduced them to him.

"Most High Prince, here are the uncles and aunts of your wife. As you know them worthy, you shall honour them accordingly."

With that he placed the right hand of Florio into the right hands of Quintilio and Mennilio. With some visible awkwardness they embraced each other and kissed on both cheeks.

As they embraced, the brothers marvelled at the resemblance to the guest who had recently left their house, but said nothing lest their puzzlement spoil the serenity of the moment. City heralds sounded their trumpets, quickly joined by other instruments in a musical welcome to all the visitors and dignitaries. A hundred doves were released at once to signify peace and renewal of friendship among all present.

Ilario then motioned to Biancofiore to come forward. When she did, he took her hand and introduced her to the relatives.

"Gentlemen and ladies, here is your niece Biancofiore."

Amid tears of joy and love, they embraced each

other many times, each marvelling at the beauty and resemblance of the new-found relatives.

It was at that moment that bells from everywhere in Roma began to knell to announce the exit of the Pope from the city in a solemn procession of religious welcome for the visitors. Riding a gold-decorated chariot pulled by four white horses, the Pope, dressed in the highest pontifical vestments, came toward them with ceremonial slowness and blessed them with fronds of palms immersed in holy water. The crowd bowed their heads and bent their knees to receive the papal blessing and to pay homage to the pope. Florio and Biancofiore did no less.

In a mass ceremony, obviously arranged with Ilario, the Pope then baptised everybody with the words, "*Ego vos omnes baptizo in nomine Patris, et Fillii, et Spiritui Sancti. Benedictio Domini descendat super vos et maneat semper. Amen.*" [I baptise all of you in the name of the Father, and of the Son, and of the Holy Ghost. May the blessing of God descend upon you and remain there forever. Amen.]

As those words were spoken, Florio looked at the brilliant sky around him, with only one large white cloud moving across and away from them. But in the cloud, he thought he saw something ominous and reproachful: the faces of the gods who had helped him in his most troublesome moments, and especially Venus and Mars. There was anger, disappointment, and sadness on their faces. Disdain, if not revenge, was almost visible in their countenances.

Florio felt a rush of guilt and remorse in his heart. But only for a brief moment. The noise of the celebration brought him out of his reverie. He turned around to see if anyone else had noticed the gods' cloud, only to meet Ascaleon staring at him. Had he?

Ascaleon answered the silent question with a nod and a weak smile of reassurance: *don't worry; things will work themselves out*, it said.

Florio certainly hoped so. He was tired of fighting with the fates, the gods, the parents.

Chapter Fifty-Four

Florio's parents were not happy. Florio's shipmates and his treasures had returned to Marmorina for over a month already, but still there was no recent news of his arrival. King Felix had spent many days, sitting in the Great Hall of the Royal Palace, looking out the crenelated parapets for any sign of galloping messengers or scouts.

What was keeping Florio in the Roman kingdom for so long? Was he in danger? Maybe the Romans were holding him prisoner, expecting a handsome tribute for his release. Maybe they were torturing him in revenge for Lellio's demise some twenty-five years earlier. Romans never forgave an affront, let alone a death, even if accidental. Could they have killed him already? They had no qualms crucifying their captives, if only to teach a lesson to anyone contemplating an attack on Roman citizens or property.

The memory of that horrible slaughter had never been dimmed by the passing of years and events. If he had only questioned the vision or asked for learned advice—Ascaleon's for one—maybe he wouldn't have… but was it really a vision? Could it have been the result of mixing red and white wines to dilute the spicy foods eaten at the banquet? Would the gods have allowed that to happen? He had always been generous with his sacrifices to them. Well, most of the times, certainly at the annual festivals. No matter. It was done.

But when would Florio come back? Could that Biancofiore girl have convinced him to stay in Roma with her relatives? She might. She had so much power over him, way too much for a woman of inferior rank.

But wait! A group of riders was coming in, carrying the standards of Spain. Must be from Florio. News at last. Good news, he hoped.

King Felix rang a bell to summon his servants. He could walk, but not quickly. Besides, he felt more stately when carried in a throne chair to meet visiting dignitaries. He wanted this to be such an occasion. Accordingly, he ordered the servants to bring the queen to the Great Hall at once.

By the time they reached it, the messengers had arrived, with Fileno in front of them. The king looked closely, but did not see his son among them. He felt a strong heart tug, but ignored it. When the queen arrived, he spoke to Fileno.

"Welcome home, Fileno. You are like a son to us. We are glad to see you back in our city, which you left so suddenly much to our displeasure. What brings you here?"

"Your son, and my lord Florio, sent me here." He

stopped as if looking for words.

"That is good, I think. But why do you hesitate? Is something wrong? Is he well?"

The queen interrupted. "How did you find each other? Wasn't he trying to destroy you for Biancofiore? Where is he?"

Fileno was now breathing heavily. It was time to play a chess game at which he was unskilled. He needed time to remember his approach.

Sensing that the young knight needed some coaxing, the king came to his help.

"No need for haste, my lady. He is obviously tired." He turned to his servants. "Bring food and ale for the noble Fileno and his companions." Then he addressed him in a fatherly tone. "You can give us all the news while sitting at the table. Conversation is always more pleasant when shared with food."

Fileno saw his opening. "Not when the news might be upsetting, my lord."

"Then tarry no longer and inform us," shouted the king impatiently now.

"As you wish. To begin with, your son is well; he is in Roma, and he will soon be home." Again, he hesitated—this time, on purpose. "With his new bride. And his new god."

The king and the queen looked at each other, their eyes dilated in wonderment and ire. King Felix glared sternly at Fileno. "We already knew about his bride. The mariners told us. What do you mean by new god?"

The queen couldn't be left out. "Did he adopt one of our Egyptian gods? None of them is new, and that would not upset us in the least."

"It's the Christian god. The one they worship in Roma. The one Biancofiore's parents were going to thank in Compostela. The one Florio will make your people worship when he is king, if only to please Biancofiore and her Roman relatives. The one he wants you to take up on his arrival, if you ever want to see him again."

The king felt another tug in his chest—this time stronger and longer. Still he had enough strength for his fury.

"So, it has come to this. A son dictates to his father, the king of the land, what to believe and how to live. Wretched fates, why did you ever give me such a son? Instead of a walking stick to lean on, he has become a yoke on my old shoulders. He left me for years to follow that girl.

"Now he has forsaken the gods that did so much for him and follow the god of our greatest enemies? Did he forget Venus who gave him magic weapons to rescue Biancofiore? And Mars who helped him battle the seneschal, and saved him in a wall of smoke from the Egyptian flames? And the old gods who first gave him directions to find that woman?

"I have raised a snake in my lap, and he has bitten

me. So be it. Go back and tell him I'll never forsake my gods to embrace those Christian detractors. Tell him too to never come before me, his greatest foe.

"I pray the gods he has abandoned allow me to see him die ignominiously. As for Spain, I would rather turn my kingdom over to a stranger —and he looked directly at Fileno—than to a son who has betrayed his father, his king, his country, and his gods."

The queen was just as perturbed by the horrible revelations, but her reasoning was not as clouded by anger as the king. She addressed him in a calming and calculated manner.

"You are right to be angered, my lord, but you are punishing the wrong person. Our son is under the spell of a powerful witch. Blinded by her pretty wiles, he behaves like a puppet. She pulls the strings; he moves. To break the spell, we need to bring him back here."

Fileno realised that his plan was already taking the shape he had hoped for. He felt entitled to an intervention.

"With all due respect, my lord, and from what I have observed while I was with them, the queen is absolutely right. It was Biancofiore who convinced Prince Florio to visit her relatives in Roma. It was she who hired the high priest Ilario to sweet-talk Florio into Christianity. He always does her bidding. She needs a man to teach her respect and obedience. Unfortunately, your son is not that man."

The queen caught the subtle inference.

"Are you that man, dear Fileno? I remember you were quite smitten yourself by that siren."

"True, your majesty. But the gods taught me a lesson the hard way. I am nobody's swain, any more. But I am your servant, ready to do your bidding."

"Enough of this chatter," interrupted the king. "What we need is action. Decisive and unrelenting until the enemy is obliterated. Heed that famous Mars-fearing general dictum: *Veni, vidi, vici.*"

"Well spoken, my lord," commented Fileno. "But even Julius Caesar had to come and see the enemy, before he could vanquish him."

King Felix looked at him with some irritation.

"And just what do you imply by that? Is he going to make himself invisible or be surrounded by a cloud again?"

"No, my lord. As I said, he vowed not to return here until you promise to become a Christian like him, and allow your subjects to do the same."

"A promise I will not make and/or keep to a renegade son!"

"Of course not, your majesty," reassured Fileno. "But I could tell him as much without your uttering a single word of promise. Once I coax him here, you will do with him as you wish."

The king looked at the queen for approval. She gave it with a smile of mutual wickedness, betting a partner in crime. But she still wondered about Fileno's motives.

"What is your stake in this affair?"

"To serve your majesties, most of all."

She waved his answer away with her hand. This was no time for courtly protocol.

"Still after Biancofiore?"

"Unfortunately, your highness reads my heart like an open missive."

The queen approved.

"After it is all over, I will tame a Roman filly to be mounted at *my* discretion."

The king approved.

Then the queen waved Fileno toward her and embraced him. In so doing, the king told Fileno, "Now let us plan some strategy."

Fileno looked around at the companions that had escorted him from Roma.

"What about them?" he asked the king.

"Aren't they your people?" wondered the king.

"No. I don't really know them," lied Fileno, much to the consternation of his escort.

"Then we have no decision to make," concluded the king.

He turned to his royal guards, pointed to Fileno's companions, and shouted: "*Archers!*"

Before any of them could take cover, a rain of arrows transfixed them to the floor.

While the king, queen, and Fileno walked away, the guards went over the heap of wailing wounded and dispatched them quickly by sword. No report of that slaughter would ever reach Florio.

By the following day, Fileno was on his way back to Roma with fresh horses and riders.

Chapter Fifty-Five

In Roma, Florio and Biancofiore were celebrating the discovery of a new family and a new faith. There were so many people to meet and talk to and visit with all day long. Distant aunts and cousins came to the city to meet the "Princess" as they chose to call her. Each had a history of a bloodline or tales of ancestors, famous or infamous, depending on which side of the family they represented. Each was eager to hear about the harrowing adventures of the two neophyte nephews in lands they would never visit, with customs or traditions they could hardly fathom.

There was curiosity mixed with bewilderment, hospitality wrought with awkwardness. After all, how do you approach a newly married, beautiful relative who would soon be the queen of Spain, who could not speak any of their dialects, and did not even have a Christian name? She was so pretty to look at, but so hard to know her like they knew everyone else in the family. And the mystery about her attracted more visitors and gave birth to more gossip and conjectures.

Gloritia had dissimilar experiences. When she first went to see her family, she was not recognised by her own father. In fact, she was told to leave because their Gloritia had died years ago in a faraway place. It was only when Gloritia named places and people she knew and pointed to portraits and heirlooms whose origins no stranger could possibly know that they recognised her. Only then they welcomed her emotionally and gratefully back into their fold. More celebrations ensued on that part of town.

But the celebrations did not last long. Ascaleon, well aware that he had reached the end of his journey, one late summer evening went to sleep forever in the eternal city where he had spent his youth studying the classics at the Latin *lyceuum* and learning the martial arts in the Hellenic *palestrae*.

His death turned family elation into public mourning, as he was honoured not only by all the people he had known, but by so many more people who had known of him.

Florio (and Biancofiore, of course) was the one most affected by his departure.

After all the mourners filed past Ascaleon where he lay in state on a purple bed in regal vestments, Florio asked all present, except for Biancofiore, to leave them alone and close the doors behind them. It was only then that he allowed himself to cry openly over Ascaleon.

"O friend, teacher, ally, and counsellor to whom my adversities were always yours, where are you now?

"Are the gods punishing me for having deserted

them? In which heaven are you dwelling? And where will I find another like you? Who will advise me to be temperate when I want to kill someone, or urge me into action when I dally in laziness? Who will encourage me in my bleakest days, or fight next to me when I can barely lift a sword? Who will seek my welfare when attacked by adversities?

"You knew all my secrets, even the ones I never told you as you taught me to read while you could read my soul. You were more than a teacher. You were my real father.

"Whose teachings will I follow now? *I know: yours.* And they will stay fixed in my heart and my mind until I come to pass on from this life. Then, dear friend and teacher, call me up there, where I hope you shall save me a space right next to you... if for no other reason but to continue our friendship in the eternal life."

Having said these words, Florio dried his tearful eyes, and exited from the room with Biancofiore at his side.

He did not see the Roman eagle perched just above the catafalque and then soaring across the temple and into the open skies.

Upon Florio's request to bury Ascaleon in the Lateran, Ilario ordered his priests to grant such a wish and to carry it out in a most stately manner. Hundreds of mourners followed the cortege, all the men first—even boys—before the wailing women, as it was the tradition of that time and place.

At the conclusion of the funeral, the family was treated by the neighbours to magnificent "consolation meals" for the following seven days—the custom born out of the belief that no family member could have the desire or the energy to prepare any meal in the midst of so much sorrow. And food, everywhere, but especially in the Italian peninsula, has forever been the most prescribed pain reliever.

Chapter Fifty-Six

It was during the last "consolation dinner" that Fileno arrived with King Felix's reply to Florio. Of course, something was lost in the translation.

Florio welcomed Fileno back, but not as warmly as before. Ascaleon's veiled warning was still in Florio's mind—indeed even more so now that Ascaleon was not around to repeat it.

"So what news do you bring us from our father?" asked Florio when they were alone.

"Sadly, not too good, my lord. Your father's health is as low as his age is high."

"I am sad to hear that. I shall hasten to his side. But first, what was his response to my petition?"

"He was not too happy to hear about your conversion, but he still wants to hear it directly from you. Only then he will believe and act upon it as you requested. But…"

"But what? Is there more to it? Speak openly. I need to know everything."

"No, my lord. I just want to impress upon you the need for a prompt return to Spain. The king's personal physician said to waste no time if you want to see your father before…"

"Before he dies? Is his condition that serious?"

Fileno just nodded gravely.

"But we need to pack provisions and our treasures, harness mules and donkeys for a convoy, hire escorts and guides for Ilario's priests. All that takes time."

"And such a convoy would move slowly. I would search for a swifter way to travel."

"My horse is no Pegasus and I am no Icarus. Do *you* have any flying magic?" Florio asked with quite a tinge of sarcasm.

Fileno held his temper in abeyance. "My modest advice would be for you and your companions to get on fast horses and leave immediately. Meanwhile, I could prepare the convoy, arrange for the safety and comfort of the ladies, and follow you soon after."

"That sounds like a well-thought-out plan. But to leave Biancofiore behind is out of the question. She will never agree to it. And neither would I—but I'll talk to her while you rest and refresh yourself." He walked toward the door. Then turned around abruptly. "I did not recognise any of my people in your escort. What happened to them?"

"Oh, nothing but a strong case of homesickness. I was a bit angry at them, but they begged the king to let them stay with the folks they had not seen in years. Some young wives would not let them out of their sight. I understood, and so did your parents."

Satisfied with the answer, Florio left the room and went to Biancofiore's chambers. He found her singing and dancing as she was packing for the trip home. Florio smiled seeing her in a radiant mood for the first time since the passing of Ascaleon.

"What makes you so happy at a time like this?" he asked her, pleased and puzzled at the same time by her unusual levity.

"Oh, I have good news for you. Did Fileno bring good news too?"

Florio did not want to cloud her joy. "You must first tell me *yours*."

"And I will please your lordship, sir," she joked. "Gloritia's sister, a worthy midwife, just confirmed that the bump on my stomach is *not* from the Roman sweet meats."

Florio cocked his head questioningly.

"I am with child. Your child. Our child. Thanks to the gods." She corrected herself. "Thank God."

Florio embraced her. "That is wonderful news... Wonderful."

His hesitation alerted her to something untold. "You don't seem very happy. Bad news from home?"

"My father is very ill. I must leave immediately, lest I never see him alive again."

"Then let's not wait a day longer. Gloritia, Gloritia. Come quick. We must leave at once."

Gloritia came running in from the kitchen.

"Leave? You are not ready. The wagons are not loaded. What's the reason for such haste, my lady?"

Florio explained. "My father. He is dying. I must go immediately, tomorrow at the most, and on the fastest horses I can buy."

Gloritia looked at him, disconcertingly. "That may be fine for you, my lord. It will not do for my lady. In her condition, it will be uncomfortable enough in a wagon. On galloping horses?" She made the sign of the cross. "Absolutely unthinkable." She looked sternly at Biancofiore. "Unless you don't want that child."

"Of course I do," protested Biancofiore. "But I also want to be with my husband."

"Exactly what your mother said, in this house twenty-five years ago. I tried to dissuade her, but... It is not my place to make decisions for my masters."

With that she bowed and left the room, her face clearly upset by the issue.

After a long silence, filled only by Biancofiore's sobs, Florio spoke.

"Gloritia is right. We can ill-afford such a risk. From now on, your travel must be safe and comfortable."

"It will be if I am with you. Don't leave me. I have a horrible premonition."

"Premonition? That's old religion stuff. Now we trust in God. But just to be safe, I will have Ilario escort your convoy. With Fileno, who knows the roads as a scout, you will be home in no time at all. After that, no more separations. I promise you, no matter what happens with my father." He touched her belly gently. "You are my family now. My only family." As he embraced her, she stopped sobbing. Florio could not see her face hardened by primal forebodings.

As he had promised, Florio made all the travel arrangements for her and her attendants. The convoy, ostensibly of pilgrims on their way to Santiago de Compostela under the tutelage of Ilario, would move only by day and through open roads, avoiding woods, narrow passes, and unguarded freeways.

At Ilario's discretion he could evangelise people along the way, but only through gentle persuasion and fraternisation with the local leaders. Any insult or perceived outrage could precipitate hostilities if not outright reprisals and certain slaughter.

"Discretion—not assertion—will be the rule for a safe passage to Marmorina," decreed Florio. He, the duke of Ferramonte, Parmenion, Messaalino and Menedon with their squires left before the end of the next day. Fast and strong Arabian horses carried them rapidly toward the lands of the king of Spain.

On their way there they inquired of returning travellers if they had any news about the king's health. To Florio's surprise, no one seemed to have heard of the king's dying. He assumed that those he encountered were not of a rank high enough to be regaled with court news, let alone updates on the king's condition. He stopped asking and continued to push his knights (and their horses) to go faster for longer distances until they reached Marmorina ten days later.

Chapter Fifty-Seven

From the first day on the road, Fileno's eyes were fixed upon Biancofiore as often and as long as his scouting duties allowed him. Of course, he was obsequious to a fault, especially when Ilario was nearby.

Oftentimes, though, Biancofiore noticed his presence around her from morning to night. Remembering well how much he had loved her, now she looked at him to detect remnants of that feeling, in spite of his avowed liege to Florio. No matter how subtle her glances, they always met his stares. She concluded that he was either spying on her or worse.

Concerned about his silent but increasing attentions toward her, she confided her fears to Gloritia.

The old nurse dismissed her anxieties.

"As a knight sworn to safeguard you, he'd lose honour if anything untoward happened to you. Don't fret about how he goes about doing it."

But Biancofiore's womanly instincts would not be quieted by Gloritia's reassurances. She began carrying a gilded dagger under her garments. At night she put it under her pillow. By day she tried to be always near someone she trusted. Mostly Ilario.

Then one morning, a week into their passage, Biancofiore walked out of her wagon to discover that Ilario and his priests were gone. Something was wrong. She called Gloritia. "Find out what happened to Ilario. He wouldn't have left without informing us."

Gloritia had the answer.

"He was told that hamlets around here haven't had a priest for years to do baptisms, marriages, funerals. And folks are slowly going back to the old ways. Ilario would have none of that. He and his priests will reconcile the villagers and then catch up with us. He told me himself."

Biancofiore had one last question. "Just how did Ilario find out about the priestless villages?"

"While scouting, Fileno was asked by some locals if any of his pilgrims were priests. When he said yes, they told him of their needs. Ilario and his people left immediately at daybreak."

"That does not bode well for us," remarked Biancofiore, her face a picture of disappointment and distrust.

Gloritia was perplexed by her attitude. "It is the Christian way to help those who seek the blessing of the Mother Church. What could possibly be wrong with that?"

Plenty, thought Biancofiore, turning away from her. She met the stare of Fileno—only it was more of a leering smile than an admirer's swoon that glowed on his face.

"I'll take good care of my charges," he promised with a sardonic glint.

Biancofiore felt a cold bodice-ripping sword violating her body.

Chapter Fifty-Eight

Florio ran his horse up the palace stairs and to the doors of the Great Hall. He dismounted and signalled to his retinue to do the same. They did and began walking with him toward the king's chambers when they were greeted by the king himself coming out of the hall.

"What manners of noblemen are you, riding horses into my palace? Have you no respect for the crown of Spain?" he shouted at them, not even recognising Florio.

Florio ran toward his father and embraced him. "Father, forgive an anxious son. I was afraid to arrive too late. No disrespect meant by me and my companions. But I am so happy to see you alert and alive." He kissed him on both cheeks.

The king pushed him away. "Who are you to call me father? And who are these invaders? Guards! Guards!"

The queen entered the room and started running toward her son, but King Felix held her back.

"Remember what Fileno told us," he whispered at her.

The guards kept smiling at Florio and at the king,

thinking that it was all a family protocol.

But Florio was not the least pleased to be treated like an intruder.

"Father, this is Florio. Don't you recognise your own son? Has the illness left you without memory?"

"What illness? My old age and my disrespectful son have failed me, but I am still sound of mind to know my son… and that is not you, not the Florio I raised and loved. That one is dead. What I have here is a usurper who abandoned his old parents for a Roman wench, his kingdom for a voyage to Egypt, and his Olympian gods for a carpenter who was crucified like a common thief. Guards!"

He pointed his right hand to them, then swung it down to direct their arrows at Florio. Nothing happened.

The guards smiled benevolently at the monarch, as to one who acts wildly after a night of libations. Shoot arrows at Prince Florio? It had to be a court game.

Florio did not see it that way.

"I *am* that same son, sire. And the fifth order of my new religion is to 'Honour thy father and mother', which I do anyway."

He moved toward the queen to embrace her, but the king drew his sword. Florio was angry and dumbfounded.

"Mother, I came as soon as I could, and I am welcomed no better than an Osman invader?"

The queen pushed her husband aside and embraced

Florio.

"Osman, Christian, Judeans—your father hates all those one-god believers—they have brought us nothing but trouble. At our age, we'll stick with the old ones. But what's all that talk about him dying?"

"*Mother!* You are the one who sent Fileno back with that dreadful news."

"We did no such thing, but we're glad you came so quickly, son. It shows where your heart is." She looked around. "And Biancofiore? Didn't she come with you?"

Florio, astounded and lost in his ruminations, could only whimper, "Fileno, Fileno," as a terrible truth began to make its way through the webs of anger and vengeance crowding his mind. He turned to his group quietly voicing his anger.

"Ascaleon was right. Fileno is a traitor. A manipulator. A conniving backstabber... and I have left him in charge of Biancofiore. What a fool I have been. What a naïve, gullible schoolboy I have been to trust such a conspirator."

His whispers were loud enough to be heard by the king.

"Fileno is a better man than a son who lets his woman tell him how to live and what to believe. But there is a remedy for that," shouted his father.

Florio came back at him with a tinge of sarcasm. "What? Send her to the stake? Sell her again? Is that how you deal with anyone who crosses you, Father?"

The king looked at him dourly. "Fileno will deal with her, saddle her and mount her. And that will suit me just fine."

The queen looked at him reproachfully. It was not what she wanted to hear.

Florio was just as incensed. "You talk about my wife as if she were an Arabian horse. What kind of father have you become to side with a schemer against your own son?"

"A captain will hang his helmsman to run a tight ship," was his stony answer.

"Then there is no room for love and compassion in this court."

"Love is irrelevant to a king. It's ale after a good meal. Power is the meal that sustains you. But you are too drunk with love and unfit to rule. Fileno is no kin, but he is a shrewd knight. I could trust him with my kingdom's regency."

Florio looked at his brooding father with more pity than disdain.

"And I wouldn't trust him with a goat. As for the kingdom, it's yours to do as you please. I wouldn't trade what I have for all the coins in your treasury." He turned to his weeping mother. "I must go back to her. I need fresh horses and a few more men. The ones I sent here will do. Can your servants find them for me?"

The queen's face turned from sorrow to horror as she looked at the king for an answer. The king started to cough and move about as if he was having trouble breathing. Florio could not understand why his simple request had caused such odd reactions.

The explanation came from the balcony. "You can find them yourself outside the city walls by the old river bed," volunteered the guards' commander.

Florio turned to him. "By the Paupers' Cemetery? What are they doing there?"

"Resting," was the laconic answer, amid raucous laughter of the entire unit.

Florio understood. He plucked a lance from one of his companions and threw it forcefully at the speaker. The lance passed halfway through his body before it stopped. The commander fell down from the balcony to the ground floor. Florio stared at the guards, daring them to respond in kind. Nobody moved. Florio and his group rode slowly out of Marmorina, pausing briefly by the unmarked graveside of their companions before they whipped their horses into a gallop. Florio's only thought: destroy Fileno.

Chapter Fifty-Nine

Fileno had only one goal in mind: possess Biancofiore. He had pined for her, loved her, and worshipped her. Now he simply lusted for her. Fully realising that he could never have her as long as she was married to Florio, he had made all the plans to separate her from her husband and protector and eliminate anyone who stood in his way to conquer the unconquerable. Now he was almost there. He had sent Ilario on a fool's errand. No farmer or shepherd had asked for a priest to perform holy rites, but he knew how fervent a priest Ilario was. It was easy to bait him into leaving Biancofiore— briefly, of course—for a major opportunity to practise his ministry of evangelisation and pastoral care.

On the way to the hamlet where he and his fellows were to tend to the priest-less flock, they were attacked by Fileno's henchmen and slaughtered like lambs for an Easter meal. The clergy's only weapons—crucifixes— did not stop the butchers. Martyrs' blood soaked the arid plains and their bodies become fodder for animals and birds of prey.

When informed by his executioners that the plan had been carried out successfully, without witnesses or survivors, Fileno summoned the pilgrims and spoke to them, easily breaking out in feigned tears before them.

"Princess Biancofiore, Lady Gloritia, I am extremely sad to announce the loss of your spiritual leader, the holy Ilario, and his venerable priests. They were ambushed and killed by pagans, I am sure, just before they reached the villages that had asked for them.

"For as much as I would like to give them a decent burial, I think that we should leave immediately and go directly to Montorio, where I have noble knights and squires who can protect us. If we stay here, we might be the next victims."

The pilgrims reacted to the horrible news with cries of anguish and terror. Some wanted to turn back to Roma. Others wanted to pray for the dead and for the living. Confusion, mixed with fear, spiked by a sense of helplessness coursed through the group. They looked to Biancofiore and Gloritia for guidance and decisions.

Biancofiore had a suggestion.

"Why don't we send couriers to Florio in Marmorina and to my family in Roma asking for protection from any attackers?"

"I already have sent two messengers to Prince Florio," Fileno reassured her. "Roma is much too far now. If we leave quietly, travel over country roads, and follow my lead, we will be safe. But I will suffer no laggards to slow our pace and no recalcitrant to endanger our convoy."

They agreed with him more out of necessity than conviction. Gloritia recited the Pater Noster. Upon its last words *"libera nos a malo"* [deliver us from evil], all answered fervently "Amen!"

Chapter Sixty

Florio whipped his horse by slamming the reins' slack from side to side, over its neck. It wasn't really necessary—as the horse was already at full gallop—but it wasn't brutal either, as the ornamental blanket under the saddle protected the skin of the animal. It was just a way—mental more than physical—to impart a sense of urgency to his steed, which would then be passed on to his companions.

It was at moments like these that he wished he could invoke his "old gods", as he called them now, for a feat of magic that could transport him instantly to Biancofiore's side. What was that he told Fileno upon hearing of his father's supposedly grave condition? Ah, yes… My horse is no Pegasus and I am no Icarus…

He could use some flying magic now. But who could provide it? He had publicly abandoned his gods, but… had they abandoned him? Were they gone forever? Didn't Ascaleon say that the gods will exist as long as people believe in them? Venus had helped and so had Mars. Could he ask one more time as to an old friend? What would be the damage? Anything to save Biancofiore…

Biancofiore reminded him of Venus. Venus and Mars, lovers like them... He wished and prayed very hard even though he knew they would not listen to him. After all, he had turned his back to them. Then something happened.

His horse, seemingly injected with extraordinary power, began going faster and faster, soon overtaking all the others... and still it went faster and then... it left the ground... and... and flew over the plains, the trees, the hills. Florio looked back and saw his companions and saw himself with them galloping on the ground and he could not understand as they disappeared when a red cloud enveloped him and his horse and transported them over the mountains and back to Italy and landed them on a country road leading to a camped caravan of pilgrims.

Chapter Sixty-One

Biancofiore was afraid, terribly afraid of Fileno. He was now following her everywhere—to the spring fountain for drinking; to the river for bathing, even if fully clothed. He came to the canopied wagon in which she slept with Gloritia. He escorted her to the rustic table set up for meals prepared by the women with wildlife killed by the men. Gloritia was always with her or nearby.

For Fileno, Gloritia was an obstacle, a nuisance—vigilant eyes that saw everything, attentive ears that heard everything, a vocal tongue that could tell everything, a closed door to the enjoyment of Biancofiore's garden of delights. Gloritia had to be silenced, removed, and eliminated. She was.

A long veil, twisted into a noose, wrapped tightly around her throat, then around her mouth, and finally around her entire face, had put an end to her life of devotion to the Julian family. It was the same veil Biancofiore had given, under royal pressure, to Fileno for his jousting tournament. It had brought victory to Fileno, embarrassment to Biancofiore, jealousy to Florio, and now death to Gloritia.

When it was all over, Fileno removed the veil from

Gloritia's face, folded it carefully in a kerchief fashion, and stashed it in his doublet pocket. He then climbed into Biancofiore's canopied wagon. She was in bed.

"Is that you, Gloritia?"

"Yes," answered Fileno in a falsetto voice that did not fool Biancofiore.

She reached for the gilded dagger under her pillow.

Fileno crawled closer, then stood to reveal himself to her. It was evening, dark, with barely enough light to make out Fileno's handsome, familiar features.

"What do you want here?" asked Biancofiore, steeling herself to hide her trepidation.

"Something I have been waiting for a long time." He knelt next to her.

Biancofiore sat up quickly and pushed him away. "Gloritia!" she screamed.

Fileno fell backward, but sprang back on his feet. "She can't answer. She's gone."

"Gloritia would never leave me. What did you do to her?"

She was slowly, quietly trying to pull the dagger out of the scabbard.

"Nothing. I kindly eased her out of her old age."

"Assassin. Murderous, vile killer," she screamed. "Help! Somebody, help me!"

Fileno sneered. "Nobody can." He turned around to point outside. "These people will help me, but obviously I don't need them."

He laughed sardonically and opened the wagon's canopy to address the pilgrims.

"We are having a little fun. Go on about your business. Go on."

Biancofiore saw her opportunity. She pulled out the dagger and plunged it into Fileno's back. It didn't go very far. The thick leather surface of his doublet took most of the strike, with only the point of the dagger cutting into his flesh. She pulled it out to strike again.

Fileno spun around in anger more than pain and took the dagger away from her.

"You want to be an Amazon? Fine, I'll turn you into one. But you'll only need one breast to be a better archer."

With that he ripped Biancofiore's tunic off her shoulders to bare her breasts. And he would have carried out the threat—having already raised the dagger to perform the horrendous act—but the beauty of her turgid orbs gave him second thoughts. He let the dagger fall from his hand to reach for her breast.

"No. Beauty is to be enjoyed, not destroyed. And you are more beautiful than Venus."

An eerie sound presaging a windstorm passed over them.

Biancofiore prayed in her mind. "Venus, help me one more time; avenge yourself on this blasphemer! I'll be forever grateful. Forever."

The wind's ululate increased and became a sinister

wailing. Fileno paid no heed to it, his lust-drunken eyes fixed on Biancofiore's charms.

Realising she was about to be raped, Biancofiore shifted to a survival role. "Be gentle with me. I am with child. A nobleman would not hurt a mother, right?"

Fileno smiled fiendishly.

"You are not a mother, and I will not hurt you. Unless you insist."

He encircled her in his arms and began kissing her furiously, erratically all over her face. Strangely, every spot he kissed turned into cold marble. In no time at all her entire face became as cold and smooth as the head of a Greek statue.

Fileno stopped kissing her, stupefied and horrified by the metamorphosis he was causing.

The wind had now become a mournful lamentation of sorts by nature or the gods. Suddenly, through the sound of the wind emerged the cadence of galloping hoofs and the neighing of frightened horses. Something ominous was assaulting their camp, something that dampened Fileno's lust and turned it into anger against the intrusion.

Standing on the wagon's rider seat, he could see his men being slashed by a horseman emerging from a cloud of dust with the fury of an enraged demon. Lightning broke through the sky, its reverberation illuminating the face of the warrior now clearly out of the cloud.

"Florio!" screamed Fileno in disbelief and rage. With one motion he kicked one of his men off his horse, mounted it, and charged toward Florio, his sword in one hand and a lance in another.

Florio saw his rival coming at him at a full gallop. He recalled Ascaleon's military teachings the night before his first duel with the seneschal. According to the first rule, *take the high ground*, he positioned himself on top of a hillock and waited for the charge. He could see Fileno's armature and manoeuvre as he approached the hill.

Do not ride your horse fast when far away from the enemy. Pick up speed when you approach him. Fileno spurred his horse into gallop immediately. The horse responded at first, but then slowed down to a trot.

Do not lower the lance first; it will foretell your move. When Fileno closed in with the lance directed at him, Florio simply pulled the rein on his horse to avoid the attack and struck Fileno in the back as he sped by. Fileno turned around, but could not see Florio clearly.

Do not go into a dusty wind; it will hinder your visibility. Florio then plunged his spurs into the horse's belly. The horse felt the pain and ran faster, but not for long. Fileno turned around, but could not see Florio because of the dust around him. He attacked anyway, aiming his lance at Florio's helmet, but it only glanced him.

Aim the lance to the throat, not the helmet, for

greater damage. Florio countered with a sword's blow to Fileno's midsection.

Low blows hurt more than high (head) blows. Fileno's pain was visible as he doubled over the neck of his horse. Florio then moved in.

Direct the chest of your horse against the shoulder of his horse to cripple it. Florio did just that. Fileno's horse collapsed under him. Fileno barely jumped off the saddle to avoid being trampled by the horse. Florio drew his sword and approached him carefully, launching some tentative strikes.

Do not strike too many blows; you tire; your sword breaks. Fileno, eager to show why he was such a jousting champion, was constantly attacking Florio. But Florio had not forgotten.

Always shield yourself, even when attacking. He parried his angry strikes with calm and confidence in his ability.

Fileno became angry and tried to distract him with taunts.

"I had my way with your Biancofiore. She is not a white flower any more. She is all wilted now. Look at her. Naked before everyone. And when I am done with you, everyone will have her." And he laughed and leered as he spoke.

Florio was tempted to look, but he remembered Ascaleon's admonishment. *Do not let screaming or other noises distract you, but keep your eyes open to all things about you.*

He answered Fileno's taunts with few, well-aimed, deliberate strikes to his arms, legs, and back.

Fileno at last realised he was in trouble. He called for his people to help him.

"Come here, you scoundrels. I have fed you and paid you well to serve me. Strike him down. Throw spears. Beat him with your pikestaffs."

Florio stared down Fileno's henchmen, while heeding his mentor's advice.

Show confidence and never fear anyone else. Fear does not kill you, but it can paralyse you.

One of them shouted back at Fileno.

"If we shoot arrows, we could hit you, my lord."

"Then throw me your shield and do what I say," he ordered him.

The man obeyed and rolled his shield toward Fileno. Fileno picked it up and raised it over his head.

For the first time Florio felt a sense of despair. A shower of arrows would definitely kill him. He looked past Fileno at Biancofiore, who stood by the covered wagon with her shoulders still bare and her hair dishevelled. It was only an instant, but long enough for Fileno to throw a gladius at him that caught him on the upper thigh. Florio gritted his teeth and tried to ignore the pain. This would not kill him. He pulled the short sword out and threw it at Fileno. It missed him.

Biancofiore raised her hands to the sky to signal a

prayer. Then she lowered the left hand forming a fist across her chest and raised her right hand to the sky as if holding a sword.

Florio understood. Invoke the help of Mars. Ascaleon's last words at the end of that military session had been, *"With your armour and sword, and me next to you, you have nothing to fear."*

So he said a mental prayer to his mentor. *I know I don't deserve this, but only you can intercede with Mars, just one last time. Do it for Biancofiore, whom you loved like your daughter.*

From the back of the wagons came a thunderous noise. As people looked in that direction, a huge shield came rolling down, shining like a star, decorated with exquisite battle scenes all over it. The shield rolled swiftly past the astonished crowd until it came to rest at Florio's feet. He picked it up easily as if it had been his shield forever.

Fileno was livid with rage. "What are you waiting for, cowards? Shoot all your arrows. Kill him."

The archers hesitated, but not for long. A rain of arrows soon descended upon Florio from all directions. Not one hit him, as the shield seemed to rotate around his arm to catch all darts and return them to the shooters. This was no ordinary shield, they decided. They stopped shooting.

The duel between the two combatants continued, but obviously Fileno was getting tired.

When your enemy tires, do not spare any blows.

Florio began to attack with renewed vehemence and alacrity, as if he had just begun to fight. But blood was flowing copiously from his thigh. He had to dispatch Fileno quickly or else. He wished his divine friend Mars were there. The wish gave him a sudden spurt of energy and a flash of Ascaleon's favourite fencing move. Florio spun around Fileno, stabbed him between his shoulder blades, and came to face him with a gladius sword. It wasn't needed.

Fileno collapsed to his knees. As he did, he took one last look at Biancofiore—this time one of untarnished love, like when they first met at the court. Slowly, painfully he pulled a bloodied veil halfway out of his doublet before he fell back, his eyes still open, but seeing nothing.

At the sight of Biancofiore's veil Florio felt a pang of old jealousy. He flipped it over with a rapid sweep of his sword and let it fall on Fileno's face. The veil became his shroud: one with his blood.

Florio turned away just in time to see two figures enter the cloud that had brought him there: a red-bearded knight with splendid armour and a beautiful lady covered by diaphanous veils.

The two looked at Florio and Biancofiore with the godspeed and melancholy expressions of friends parting for the last time. No matter where they would go, they would be bonded for eternity.

The gods disappeared within the cloud. And the cloud disappeared into the twilight.

Thunder echoed in the moonless sky. The night came suddenly, reverently filled with stars.

EPILOGUE

Ten days later, when the sun arose from behind the gentle hills of Montorio, a pilgrims' caravan was slowly making its way toward Santiago de Compostela.

Florio and Biancofiore had decided to complete her parents' unfulfilled vow as a cogent tribute to the serendipity of their untimely deaths, which had brought them together. In their memory, the coming baby would be named Lellio if a boy, Julia if a girl.

But before they crossed into northern Spain, they stopped at a rural temple, at the edge of a lush forest. There they sacrificed two wild boars, one to Venus and one to Mars. Just so.

If their guides had gone up the hill at the end of that forest, they would have observed, in the distant plains, a sea of infantry and cavalry troops moving north toward the Pyrenees.

It was the Umayyad army of Abd-er Rahman, Spanish Muslim governor, moving into France to spread his new-founded religion. A month later, in October 732, that seasoned army was confronted at Tours by a Frankish army led by Charles Martel, who positioned his infantry on a high, wooded plain, thus forcing the Saracen cavalry to charge uphill and... be defeated.

Ascaleon would be proud of such a tactical manoeuvre.

Charles Martel would be Charlemagne's grandfather.

CPSIA information can be obtained
at www.ICGtesting.com
Printed in the USA
LVHW110108071220
673514LV00005B/155

9 781784 657611